The Rover Bold

Viking Roots Medieval Romance Saga

~Book One

ANNA MARKLAND

Cover Art by Steven Novak

For my darling Katie,
and all who seek a better life.

TABLE OF CONTENTS

FOREWORD.

Readers of my books have come to know and love members of the Montbryce family. **The Rover Bold** travels back in time to introduce their Norse ancestors.

Even if you aren't acquainted with the Montbryces, the FitzRams and the Sons of Rhodri, you'll enjoy this adventurous tale of Viking rovers who set sail for Francia in the tenth century in search of a better life.

That much is historical fact. Their leader, Hrolf Ganger, became the famous Rollo, founder and first Duke of Normandy (named of course for the North Men) and a direct ancestor of William the Conqueror. This is the fictitious story of a man who came with Rollo, a *Rover Bold* destined to establish a powerful dynasty of his own.

PART ONE

THE END

"He who can't defend his wealth must die,
or share with the Rover Bold."
~St. Olaf

BITTER TRUTHS

Møre, Norway, Autumn 910 AD

"Our harvests have failed again," the Chieftain declared, legs braced, meaty hands fisted on hips—a man too big for any horse to bear. His booming voice echoed in the silent Ringhouse and reached his audience despite the keening of the icy wind blowing off the already freezing fjord.

Standing alone among his kinsmen and neighbors summoned to listen to the man who had led them for a generation, Bryk Gardbruker surveyed the bedraggled and hungry people of Møre. The dire pronouncement had not come as a surprise.

He unfolded his arms and sauntered over to take up a position beside his one surviving brother. Alfred stood guard at the door of the root cellar where their meager crop was stored.

Legend had it apples were the food of the dead, but the small, bitter fruit Bryk and his brother had salvaged during the earliest blizzard in living memory was one of the few sources of food in the entire settlement.

Alfred shifted his weight. "Look at them glaring. They know we've no intention of hoarding the fruit, but careful rationing will have to be enforced if any of us hope to survive until spring.

"Ice fishing will be the only other means of sustenance, and I for one don't want to eat *lutefisk* all winter."

Bryk grimaced, the cloying taste of lye already in his mouth. He fixed his gaze on Hrolf Ganger, the chieftain, son of Rögnvald, first *jarl* of Møre. No one would make a move without his approval.

Hrolf raked a hand through windblown hair as white as the snow in which he stood. "Our livestock and many of our boats are lost, swept away by last month's storm tide."

Bryk exchanged a glance with Alfred, remembering the desperate struggle to survive the brutal storm that had swept in from the sea. Many had perished, including their younger brother, Gunnar. Homes had been destroyed. The roof of the once impressive Ringhouse was gone. They gathered within its battered walls, but it no longer shielded them from the elements.

Alfred must have read his thoughts. "The gods were evidently dissatisfied with the sacrificial ox buried in the foundations."

The sheltered inland glade where the Gardbruker family's trees grew had saved them from being uprooted. Villagers had clung to the gnarled trunks of his trees in the ferocious winds.

Bryk narrowed his eyes. Hrolf was wise, a folk hero celebrated among his people for more than twenty years of successful raids, mainly into Francia. *Skalds* sang of his exploits around many a hearth.

He never rode, but even on foot he was intimidating. He had played a role in the year-long siege of Paris, unsuccessful only because the King of Francia finally gathered an army and marched to relieve the wealthy city. No battle was fought— Hrolf maintained the Vikings gained more by agreeing to terms.

"Next he'll tell us again of the outrage of the Parisians who had defended the city when King Charles the Fat stopped short of attacking the Viking besiegers," Bryk said sarcastically.

Alfred chuckled. "And how instead he allowed the Norsemen to sail further up the Seine to raid Burgundy, which was in revolt against him, as well as promising a handsome payment. Hrolf harried Burgundy, *where fine crops are raised and the best of wines made.*"

Bryk coughed into his fist to hide his amusement at Alfred's excellent imitation of Hrolf's frequent boast. "I often wonder why Ganger bothered to return to Møre," he said under his breath.

Alfred snorted. "Judging by the permanent grimace on the face of his concubine, I'd guess she wished he hadn't dragged her with him."

Bryk grinned, rolling his eyes. "Poppa loves to remind everyone she is a high born Frankish woman captured in a raid on Bayeux."

In the intervening years Hrolf had continued to go a-viking to Francia, to the coasts of Ireland and Scotland, and other far-flung places, always returning with plunder. Bryk had accompanied him on many of these journeys until—

"There is but one thing to be done," Hrolf declared. "We must leave this cursed place. Start afresh in a new land, a kinder land."

Only the mocking call of a lone seagull soaring on the wind above the timbers of the damaged roof broke the utter silence that greeted this proclamation.

Murmurs of dissent began as barely audible whispers, gradually growing louder until Hrolf raised his hand. "We will rebuild our boats and sail again to Francia." He paused, his steely gaze surveying his people. "I know the way."

A few chuckled. Poppa's face brightened.

Without much effort he'd succeeded in calming the crowd. He had reassured them. They trusted and admired him.

Bryk didn't.

Hrolf's sister had died of grief after he'd shunned her—for being married to Bryk. Myldryd had taken their unborn child to the grave.

"I suspect this sudden desire to leave Norway has a lot to do with Hrolf's falling out of favor with King Harald Fairhair," he spat through gritted teeth, pushing aside the bitter memories. Intent on raising the Chieftain's ire, he cupped his hands to his mouth and shouted, "What will we do in Francia? Most of us are farmers and fishermen, not warriors."

Hrolf's gaze bore into him as a hush fell over the crowd. "If you're a Viking, you're a warrior. We will raid and plunder and claim the land as our own. There are noble Frankish families with daughters aplenty who will make excellent brides for conquering warriors."

Grunts of approval rippled through the crowd as unmarried men puffed out their chests.

Hrolf rode the tide of growing enthusiasm. "The Franks have become soft. We will mow them down like the bitter wind destroys budding flowers."

Many thrust fists into the air, roaring their approval.

Hrolf restored quiet with a brief wave of the hand. "Hundreds from neighboring villages and settlements will wish to join us. Odin has revealed this to me. Our destiny as Norsemen lies in the bountiful land of the river Seine. There will even be a place for men who grow apple trees."

Bryk shrugged off the insult. At one time the settlement's second most celebrated warrior, he'd turned his back on plundering and raiding, sickened by the mindless barbarism. Bringing home spoils was one thing; bloodletting for sport was another. His brothers had welcomed him to the family farm. Hrolf wasn't the only man present who thought little of him. His countrymen considered him a coward. *Skalds* no longer sang of his heroic deeds.

THE FOUNDLING

Rouen, Francia, Spring 911 AD.

A black booted toe poked Cathryn's chapped hand. "You missed this section."

No need to look up from where she knelt to know who had spoken. She took a deep breath, praying for humility. "I beg forgiveness, *Mater*."

She remained on her knees, tightened her reddened fingers around the rough wooden brush, and rescrubbed the already clean part of the elaborate mosaic flooring Reverend Mother had indicated.

Seemingly satisfied, her superior swept off, clucking like a hen. When she deemed it safe, Cathryn sank back on her haunches and raised her head in time to see the black robed *Mater* swoop into the chapel like a carrion crow. She cringed as she looked across the vestibule to her red-faced friend Kaia, who had also ceased scrubbing. "*Mater* will surely find some other postulant to pick on in that holy place," she whispered, hooking a finger into the tight coif under her chin.

They both quickly resumed their task when *Mater* suddenly bustled out of the chapel only to disappear into the refectory.

"She's full of fire and brimstone this morning, and the sun isn't up yet," Kaia complained. "She delights in finding fault."

Cathryn heaved a heavy sigh. Life at the abbey convent dedicated to Saint Catherine of Alexandria had certainly changed since the promotion of Sister Bruna. "If only *Mater* Silvia still lived. She loved us."

Kaia too sighed. "And we loved her. She would never have had us on our knees at this hour scrubbing tiles. If such treatment continues I shall ask Papa to send me elsewhere for my education."

Cathryn came to her feet, inspecting the heavy linen apron. *Mater* would impose some burdensome penance if it became soiled. Kaia might have the wherewithal to effect changes in her station, but Cathryn had no such option. She had lived in the abbey since birth, a foundling left in a basket at the door. There was no life outside its walls. No one cared.

Feeling the need to justify the benefits of the convent, she said, "We are safe here. Unlike many Rouennais, we've never been forced to flee from Vikings. Our position atop this hill has saved the community from the intermittent raids that have gone on along the Seine for nigh on thirty years."

She had the sinking feeling her words sounded like one of *Mater* Bruna's lectures.

Kaia snorted, confirming her fears, but she had frightened herself with talk of Vikings and couldn't seem to stop. "Pillaging the many churches on islands offshore from the town has kept the marauders busy. The cathedral has been plundered often, but never totally destroyed. They tend to stay within easy reach of the river and flee quickly with their treasure trove.

"*Mater* Silvia told me Rouen has been a Frankish city since the rule of Clovis four hundred years ago. She said most in the town seem resigned to the attacks since King Charles the Senseless provides no protection."

Kaia smiled at the nickname the Franks had bestowed on their king and seemed more inclined to listen. "My father says many locals are descended from former pirates from Northern lands or from Britain who settled in the valley of the Seine. They are farmers for the most part.

"Villages closer to the sea have suffered years of foreign attacks. I've overheard Papa tell horrific tales of fire and carnage, people massacred, towns half destroyed. It's common practice for many to disappear into the remote areas of the countryside at the onset of summer."

Cathryn wondered why a nobleman would expose his daughter to such lurid accounts. Keeping an eye on the long hallway leading to the refectory, she shuddered, thinking herself blessed she'd never set eyes on a Viking. Being shut away from the world atop a steep hill had its advantages.

They got off their knees and she helped Kaia lift her bucket of dirty water. Her friend was frail and would have difficulty managing the task alone. Bearing the weight between them, each with one hand on the handle, they hefted the vessel towards the rear door of the kitchens.

Cathryn would never openly criticize her superior. It wouldn't be Christian. "This is the only home I've ever known. I was happy growing up here under the tutelage of *Mater* Silvia. She was a mother to me."

Kaia swiped the back of her free hand across her forehead. "It was she who taught you to read?"

Cathryn shoved open the heavy door and they picked their way to the ditch behind the kitchens in the pre-dawn darkness. It was hard not to giggle as they hopped about trying not to get splashed by mud as the water cascaded into the ditch.

"Read and write," Cathryn confirmed. "She also nurtured my love of learning other languages, and shared with me the art of illuminating manuscripts. *Mater* Bruna can never take that away from me. I will persevere with her, as Saint Catherine persevered through her trials and tribulations with Emperor Maxentius. This is where I belong."

As they made their way back inside, Cathryn pondered the future. She was certain it was God's will she spend her life emulating Saint Catherine. The nuns had bestowed the saint's name on her.

But doubt sparked briefly when she reached the vestibule. A grim-faced *Mater* Bruna stood by her bucket of dirty water, arms folded, tapping her foot. It was an inescapable truth— Saint Catherine's perseverance had led to her martyrdom.

NO GOING BACK

Braced against the sea chest on which he sat, Bryk raised and lowered his oar rhythmically, slicing into the water, one of fifty men helping to drag the long, narrow ship forward.

Hrolf stood at the steering oar, turning his wind-reddened face from time to time on his crew. Next to him stood his son, Vilhelm. The boy sailed with the men despite Poppa's protests that at ten years of age he was too young. She thought he should be with her in one of the boats filled with women and children, elderly folk and the thralls who plied the oars.

Bryk had to grudgingly admit the man had been right. Many flocked to leave harsh lives in Norway. Their warship was one of a hundred in the fleet they had labored to build and repair, forced by the brutal winter to commandeer the Ringhouse for the purpose.

They had stripped the forests and salvaged wood from the community structure. The fires of the smithy had burned hot and long to forge new iron rivets and reshape old ones.

As they rowed away from Møre, Bryk fixed his gaze on the smoldering rubble of the gathering place his people had been justifiably proud of. He knew every man on board was swearing the same oath. They might never return, but they would never forget the land of their birth.

Many had balked at Hrolf's insistence his Frankish wife teach them a few words of her language after their work was done each day. Bryk had welcomed the opportunity to listen in the near darkness to the foreign tongue roll off the woman's lips. In a new land, such knowledge would be an advantage.

He suspected he'd been chosen for this crew so his chieftain would have opportunities to goad him, but that had not happened. Hrolf maintained his disdainful demeanor, but had declared, "Seldom will a voyage go well if the men are at odds. We are all bound by the law of an army united."

Bryk had to grudgingly admire the wit of a man who never rode having named his ship the *Seahorse*.

It had been a long journey, much of it across open sea from Møre to the western kingdom of the Franks—long and cold in early spring. Over and over he'd counted the number of squares of fabric that made up the sail until he knew in his sleep how many red and how many white the women had woven and plaited and sewn together.

They'd felt the biting chill as they sailed south, hugging the coast of Norway, keeping an eye on the brass weathervane atop the mast. They passed Bergen and Stavanger, then kept far out from shore until they reached Jutland.

They'd avoided getting too close to the misty Danish coast, preferring not to make use of the drinking horns every man carried slung on a lanyard across his body. The sound of a strident foghorn carried for miles over water.

However, they pulled in at Ribe to trade furs, honey and beeswax for weapons. Some of the older slaves were sold off, Hrolf declaring they were dead weight.

As they journeyed south, the sun's rays grew stronger every day and the wind seemed less biting. Cautious optimism took root in Bryk's heart. Tucked away safely in his sea chest alongside his sharpened *Stridsøkse* were seeds and rootstocks from the apple trees. His brother's chest held the same treasure.

Alfred, seated next to him, was finding the voyage difficult. Seven years older than Bryk, he'd been a farmer all his life. He was no stranger to manual labor, but the oar and the coarse horsehair and elk leather ropes had raised angry welts on his palms. He fretted for his wife and ten children.

It was a blessing Gunnar had been the one swept away. He was unmarried and had no children, except for a son born of his thrall.

"Jutland passed," Hrolf had yelled two days ago, his hands cupped to his mouth. "From here everything belongs to the Franks."

Now Alfred frowned. "Surely any people strong enough to conquer and hold so vast an empire are capable of mustering armies far larger than our force."

Bryk sought to reassure him. "Hrolf knows what he's doing. He plans to strike deep within the heartland of the Franks."

He hoped his voice didn't betray his fear that the boldness might prove to be dangerous folly. "By day, we've sailed out of sight of land so they don't become aware an invasion fleet is making its way down their coast."

Only at night had they anchored in hidden coves or along sandy beaches. Hrolf did indeed know the way.

It irked that he was now defending the man who had treated his wife cruelly. "Hrolf hopes to strike the first blow against the western Frankish kingdom before their king has time to gather an army. He loves to remind us that the run of the game is determined by the first move. You'd think we were playing *hnefatafl*."

Alfred shook his head. "But every morning we've landed men to forage for animals and winter crops. Surely the loss of the livestock and provisions they've brought back has alerted someone?"

He shrugged away his brother's worries. "We have to eat. It wasn't possible to bring enough provisions to feed everyone. But pirate raids are common along any coast. Hrolf doesn't believe it will have caused too much alarm. And you have to admit your belly is fuller than it has been in a while."

Alfred grunted his agreement.

Hrolf changed course suddenly, heading closer to land, away from the rest of the fleet. He signaled for the *Kriger* to follow the *Seahorse*.

"We must be getting close," Bryk said.

As they came in sight of land, Hrolf ordered a halt. "Armor," he shouted.

The rowers pulled in their oars, and those who had armor took it out of their sea chests, along with their weapons. Bryk thanked the gods he hadn't got rid of his mail shirt when he'd abandoned warmongering. Alfred, who had no armor, helped him don it once he'd pulled it out of its sealskin bag.

"Lash shields," Hrolf yelled. Alfred jumped immediately to fasten his brother's shield to the rack along the side of the ship.

Bryk accepted that his brother was dependent upon his protection.

"Is a battle at hand?" Alfred asked nervously.

"No," he replied, hefting his *stridsøkse*, then placing the heavy weapon next to his sea chest where it would be accessible. "I suspect we'll go scouting first."

Hrolf braced his legs. "We are nearing the mouth of the Seine, the mighty river that flows out from the heart of West Francia. We don't want to miss it. The fleet will wait out of sight for our signal while we search for the river's mouth."

"Why armor if we are only looking for a river?" Alfred asked.

Bryk didn't want to alarm his kind and gentle brother, but he had to be forewarned. "This is the land of the enemy," he said. "Uncertainty lies ahead. Would you track a wolf threatening your sheep without arming yourself?"

Alfred shook his head, looking anxiously out to sea, then back to shore.

The *Seahorse* hugged the coastline, its sail lashed. In the early afternoon the land curved away to the east. Hrolf signaled to the *Kriger* to pull alongside. When the ship was within hailing distance, he called to its captain. "Tormod, row out to the fleet," he said. "Tell them we have located the estuary. They should look for our camp among the islands in the delta. On the morrow we'll head downriver."

The mouth was too wide for them to see the opposite bank and the water was choppier than out at sea. Gradually the river narrowed and they encountered sandbars, and low, grassy islands. The water turned brown. They slowed down as a sailor next to Hrolf threw out a weighted line, checking the depth.

As they neared a large island Bryk recognized, Hrolf swung the ship sharply and she slid sideways in the water the last few feet. He called for a halt and the anchor was dropped. In five days, they had reached Francia.

THE CHOSEN ONE

A summons to *Mater* Bruna's office after the observance of Terce meant only one thing. Cathryn was to be punished for something. Time would tell what. Despite her prayerful entreaties to Saint Catherine, the persecution continued.

Upon receiving permission to enter the cramped room she was surprised to see a smile on her Superior's normally scowling face.

She was further astonished to be invited to sit in one of the well-upholstered chairs. A pang of regret twirled in her belly. She had spent many happy hours in this same seat soaking up the knowledge and wisdom that poured from *Mater* Silvia.

She sat politely, gripping the wooden arms, her back rigid. When *Mater* stared accusingly at her white knuckles, she nervously laced her fingers together in her lap.

Should she look at *Mater*, or keep her eyes downcast as she'd been reminded since childhood? She decided to fix her gaze on her hands.

"You have been chosen," the elderly nun declared, her mouth settling back into its usual tight moue.

Having no idea what was coming next, Cathryn deemed it wise to remain silent.

"Do you not wish to know for what you have been chosen?"

She risked a quick glance at her tormentor. "I trust in the Lord and Saint Catherine that whatever it is—"

"Yes, yes," the nun interrupted with a dismissive wave. "You're to go to Jumièges."

A maelstrom of thoughts whirled through Cathryn's head. From what she'd heard, the town was a mere ten miles distant, but it was far enough to escape Bruna's tyranny. However, the abbey at Jumièges had been destroyed by Viking marauders nigh on seventy years before, and according to rumor the rebuilding was by no means complete. Why was she being sent there? How would she travel? Was she to go alone? One thing was for certain. Travel was risky. Cathryn had never ventured further than to walk to the cemetery behind the abbey.

Saint Catherine pray for me.

"But what of Vikings?" she asked nervously.

"Too early in the year. They come in the summer, if at all. There have been no raids for several years. Your work illuminating manuscripts has come to the attention of the Archbishop of Rouen," *Mater* said, her voice edged with jealousy. "He wishes you to instruct the small community being reestablished in Jumièges. They are copying damaged manuscripts."

Again Cathryn was torn. It was work she loved, but—

"You will leave on the morrow on a trading ship bound for the sea. They will take you as far as Jumièges."

Cathryn could no longer contain her thoughts. She had only ever glimpsed the mighty river from the cemetery. "Down the Seine?"

Mater looked at her with disdain. "Of course. Do you suppose a ship can travel by road? Be ready at dawn."

A NEW LAND

A damp mist crept in from the sea as the Viking horde gathered on the island after the rest of the fleet followed the *Kriger* into the mouth of the Seine. Happy sounds of families reunited after the long voyage filled the air. Pots and pans clanked as women set about preparing for the foragers to return.

Bryk chuckled as Alfred strolled by with his youngest atop his broad shoulders and the rest of his brood clustered around his legs. His nieces and nephews called out to him. *"Onkel Bryk."*

He returned their waves with mixed feelings. He loved Alfred's boisterous children, but they reminded him keenly of his own loss.

Hrolf called a council of captains from other boats. They gathered round a bonfire near the shore. Bryk was not invited to the inner circle, but noted bitterly that Hrolf offered tumblers of his family's *eplevin* to the captains. Even young Vilhelm was allowed a taste. The Gardbrukers had been given no choice but to watch Hrolf load their entire stock of the apple wine aboard his own ship.

Bryk sat cross-legged on the fringe, huddled into his woolen cloak, ready to hasten back to the longboat once the meeting concluded. Canvas shelters were reserved for the women and children. Most of the men would have to sleep on the damp grass, and he didn't intend to be one of them. His personal thrall wouldn't be able to hold his place for long.

The chieftain climbed aboard his boat, one hand on the neck of the carved seahorse at the prow. His voice carried over the crackle of the flames as he held his wooden tumbler high. "This has been a long journey, and it's good to set our feet on solid ground again."

This statement was greeted with loud laughter and agreement, but no one sipped their wine, waiting for their leader to take the first drink in the new land.

"The gods smiled on us, and only three of our number perished on the way."

Alfred elbowed Bryk. "Aye, three drunken fools we're better off without."

Bryk remained silent, thinking of the three families facing an uncertain future without a protector.

Still Hrolf's tumbler remained aloft. Several men licked their lips. "We lost no boats!"

There was a rousing cheer.

Hrolf continued once the noise had quieted. "We are a strong and determined force. However, as many have observed, the Franks can muster a large army to rout us. Surprise and swift action will be the keys to success. We must strike before they have time to react."

"But if we sail upriver, we will be going further away from the sea," Captain Tormod said hesitantly.

Tormod had echoed what every Norseman felt in his bones. The sea offered safety, a means of escape. A Viking rarely ventured far inland in foreign climes.

Hrolf narrowed his eyes and lowered his tumbler. "This is true, but we must have courage to forge deep in their territory and take what we can to strengthen our bargaining hand. Once we take Rouen, the roads left by the Romans will give us access to vast areas."

Murmurs of confusion and discontent greeted this pronouncement.

Hrolf cleared his throat. "We are outnumbered. We will take what we want and use it to pry concessions from the King of the Franks. Traders to our lands have told of the challenges he faces from factions within Francia. They call him Charles the Senseless."

Laughter greeted this revelation.

Hrolf laughed with them, but then grew serious again. "His army is weak and he will welcome a bargain if he thinks we can be of use to him. In the past we've often extracted *geld* ransoms to leave communities in peace. The goal now is to wrest land where we can settle. There is no going back."

At last he took a long swig of his wine. The captains watched for a moment, then broke into loud cheering and drained their own tumblers.

Bryk leaned towards his brother. "The man has charmed them again, and with our wine."

LA RUSSE

Cathryn was relieved not to be the only nun making the journey to Jumièges. However, as their meager belongings were being stowed aboard the *Bonvent*, she was forced to acknowledge that *Mater* had assigned two women as companions who would be more of a liability than a blessing.

Sister Ekaterina squinted at everything and spoke the Frankish tongue with a heavy foreign accent. The exact place of her birth on the eastern plains was unknown. She was so old it was rumored she'd been alive when the relics of the blessed saint had been discovered on Mount Sinai in the Year of Our Lord Eight Hundred. She was reputed to be the only one of the community who had actually lived at the Monastery of Saint Catherine, built over the site where the aromatic relics were unearthed. She was fondly referred to by the nuns as *La Russe*.

The third member of the group was her friend Kaia, a young woman from a wealthy family who was so frail she had to be carried up the steep ramp by a grimy sailor, all the while fanning her face with her hand, nose wrinkled in disgust.

Cathryn suspected that if anything untoward happened to Kaia, *Mater* would somehow make sure the blame fell squarely on her shoulders.

She marveled at how the woman had convinced Kaia's family to allow her to undertake this risky journey.

Head held high, Cathryn climbed up the ramp, terrified of losing her balance on the flimsy plank that had no railing. After one unsettling glance at the dark water below, she resolved to keep her eyes on the heavens.

Another sailor gripped Ekaterina's hands and walked backwards up the ramp, guiding the elderly nun. Despite her advanced years and deteriorating eyesight, she was always smiling, chattering away in a language all her own. Perhaps not being able to properly see the evils of the world was a blessing.

Smoothing the folds of her habit, Cathryn took in her new surroundings. The ship was broad in the beam, its sail furled. There was a raised deck in the rear with a long wooden apparatus fixed to the side of the boat. She assumed this must be for steering.

The men of the *Bonvent* appeared to be busy preparing for departure, but she was uncomfortably aware of their hostile gazes. She looked around, wishing someone would direct them to their cabin.

A tall, bearded man with cleaner clothing than the rest of the crew approached them. "*Mes soeurs*," he said politely, pointing to a tattered canvas canopy stretched between the mast and the side of the ship. "I am Capitaine Vranche. We have provided shelter—in case of rain."

Cathryn's spirits fell as she eyed the threatening skies and the weathered canvas. "There is no cabin?" she asked.

The corners of Vranche's mouth twitched slightly.

Kaia swayed alarmingly.

Ekaterina gazed about, still smiling.

"Alas, dear Sisters," Vranche replied, "my humble ship offers no such amenity. Forgive me, I must see to preparations for departure."

He stalked off abruptly, leaving Cathryn with no option but to shepherd the other two into the shelter.

Kaia sank down sullenly onto one of the large cushions and curled her knees up to her chest.

"At least they've provided us with cushions," Cathryn said in an effort to lighten the tension.

"*Da!*" *La Russe* exclaimed breathlessly as Cathryn eased her down.

"I suppose," Kaia replied, still pouting. "But this isn't what I'm used to."

Cathryn sat beside her and took her hand. "We must look upon this as an adventure. We have been called to do God's work. He will protect us."

Despite her professed calm, Cathryn's heart was racing. Deep within, she had a troubling sense that some life-changing event would happen on this journey.

The boat lurched as it was freed from its moorings. Kaia put her forehead on her knees. Ekaterina twisted her wizened face into a grin as she turned her face to the wind and exclaimed, "*Da!*"

WILD HORSES

To his surprise, Bryk was appointed leader of a scouting party the next morning with strict instructions to find horses.

"Once we have pack animals," Hrolf declared, "raiding parties can travel fast and wreak havoc on the Franks quickly. We rendezvous this night just past the first oxbow bend in the river, on the north bank. If memory serves, it will take three hours to row there."

Bryk suspected he'd been chosen because he had armor and a reputation as a warrior. The five men assigned to him knew, as he did, that the chieftain required beasts of burden for treasure trove, not for men to ride. Vikings were foot soldiers.

They waded across the narrow strip of water between the island where they had camped and the riverbank to the south. The *Seahorse* ferried another scouting party to the opposite bank.

After an hour slogging through wet, boggy terrain, dogged by persistent flies, Bryk's group came across a handful of wild horses. The beasts looked up lazily from their grazing as he motioned his men to crouch. They watched for long minutes. It was evident the animals were aware of them.

"It appears they don't have much contact with people. They're curious, but not afraid," he said.

Young Sven Yngre frowned. "How will we capture them?"

Bryk smiled, recalling his youth when he and his father and brothers had roamed Norway looking for horses for the farm.

"Be calm," he explained. "If a horse senses you're nervous, it will scare him off. Watch me. I'll approach their leader sideways so he won't feel threatened. And never stare right into a wild horse's eyes or he'll think you're a predator."

Rope in hand, talking quietly, he sidled towards the beast that appeared to be the dominant male.

He stopped a few yards away. "You're a fine looking horse," he lied. "Magnificent indeed. Shiny coat, strong legs."

He inched his way towards the animal and slowly put out his hand to touch its neck.

It snorted, stamping one foot, then another, but didn't move away. The other horses stood stock still, watching, blonde tails twitching. Bryk talked on in a calm and soothing way. He petted the wild creature's neck. He let it smell his hand. "You're getting to know me," he crooned.

As he was about to ease the rope around its neck, it shied, snorting at another horse that had suddenly trotted up, seemingly from nowhere.

Now here was a horse! The newcomer nuzzled his hand, seemingly jealous of the first beast that it shouldered out of the way. It was several hands higher than the other horses, and gelded!

The other men had come to their feet, mouths agape. Bryk motioned them away. "Feral," he told them.

This good fortune augured well. He gave thanks to Odin's horse, Sleipnir. The brown gelding seemed to be the dominant horse, and must have been ridden at some time. It showed no fear. If he captured it, the others might follow.

He chattered on and on, patting the horse's neck, chuckling at the way the beast relished his attentions. "You've missed being with people, haven't you?"

The animal almost roped itself, and within half an hour they were leading a string of five horses across marshy plains and through forests en route to the rendezvous.

They reached the bend in the Seine after several hours, their boots waterlogged, leg wraps and woolen hose soaked, feet frozen. He had an urge to peel off his heavy mail-shirt and cast it into the deepest bog he could find.

He contemplated the river, shrugging off the discomfort. He'd been colder and wetter before. The Seine was narrower than near the mouth, but he recalled that the waters flowed swiftly here. Their comrades were on the opposite bank approximately a hundred yards away. They'd have to swim across. He was confident the gelding would accept a rider, but the wild horses would balk.

Suddenly he was shivering. Vikings lived on the sea, but few were strong swimmers, and Bryk was no exception. They had to trust the horses would keep them above the water. He had no intention of drowning in a muddy river. How would he ever find his way to Valhalla?

The apprehensive looks on the other men's faces as they urged the reluctant beasts to the sandy bank told him they were thinking the same thing. He pushed away the niggling suspicion that none of these young men had ever ridden a horse.

"Mount at the last moment," he urged them. "Let's hope they'll be more nervous about the water."

Bryk led the way on the gelding, filled with a resentful feeling Hrolf would claim the handsome beast—simply as a possession since he never rode.

The water deepened quickly. He sensed the moment his horse hesitantly allowed the water to keep it afloat. He gave the animal its head and soon it was swimming confidently. He glanced behind. The other riders were not faring as well, their mounts obviously terrified of the deep water. Sven Yngre struggled for control, but suddenly slid into the cold water. His horse turned, headed back to the shore they had just left, Sven clinging to its mane.

The remaining horses seemed to sense the panic in the air. They halted close to mid stream, refusing to move despite the frantic shouts of the riders. If they didn't start swimming soon, they'd be swept downriver.

Movement from behind drew his attention. The *Seahorse* was approaching at speed from the other bank. Bryk feared the boat might make matters worse.

With some difficulty, he turned his own horse in time to see Sven lose his grip and slip under the water.

Gritting his teeth, Bryk motioned frantically to the Vikings in the boat. "Save Sven," he yelled. "I'll see to the horses."

The longboat glided past him, but he didn't look away, his attention fixed on the men.

His mount seemed to sense what he intended. It swam strongly to the last horse in the group then continued on back to the bank. The wild horses followed until all were safely back on the sandy shore they'd left minutes before. Bryk slid from his horse, reached his arms around its neck and rested his forehead on the animal's. "Thanks be to Freyja we found you. I name you *Fisk*, for you surely swim like a fish."

Fisk nickered as if in agreement.

Panting, soaked to the skin, Bryk looked out to the river.

Hrolf stood braced at the helm of the *Seahorse* just offshore. "We have him," he bellowed, pointing into the bow where Sven huddled. Bryk was relieved he wouldn't have to explain the death of her only son to Sven's grieving mother.

"Stay on that side," Hrolf hollered. "We must follow the river. It winds back and forth, but you can go overland, due east to where it narrows. We'll meet again near the town there."

Bryk had never ventured this far inland, but he recalled something of Hrolf's tales. "Jumièges?"

"*Ja!* Jumièges. It's a good place to start raiding."

ILLUMINATING

The reconstruction of the devastated abbey at Jumièges was only partially complete, but it was immediately clear to Cathryn it would be a magnificent edifice. The Abbot had welcomed them with kindness, seemingly elated at having an "expert" in their midst. She'd been allotted a small working area within the confines of the library, the only part of the abbey that had been completed thus far. Even the kitchen was a makeshift affair of partial walls and canvas.

Two monks were assigned as her pupils. Brother Javune, a handsome youth from Rouen, was eager to learn. The other, an older man named Brother Sprig, was not. He evidently resented being tutored by a female and refused to speak to her during the lessons.

"He's from Neustria," Javune whispered, as if that explained the rudeness.

After a sennight of trying without success to elicit some verbal response from Sprig, Cathryn decided this was yet another test of her worth as an adherent of Saint Catherine. Since Javune held promise, and Sprig's talents were mediocre, she carried on as if nothing were amiss.

Ekaterina went off to the river each day early in the morning, rarely returning until dusk. Cathryn supposed the woman spent her time in meditative prayer.

For the first two days Kaia wandered from place to place, always sullen, bothered by a hacking cough she'd developed on the boat. On the third day, she meandered into Cathryn's workplace and set eyes on Javune. From that day forth she became a frequent visitor and her cough seemed to miraculously disappear.

Javune's face reddened whenever Kaia happened by and leaned over his work, feigning interest.

After a fortnight, Cathryn decided to speak to Kaia. Not only was her behavior sinful, Javune's work was suffering as a result, and Sprig's smirking face showed his increasing disdain.

"He's a monk," she whispered to her friend between gritted teeth as they huddled together for warmth in their draughty cell after the evening meal. "And you are a postulant."

"*Da!*" Ekaterina interjected from the pallet where she lay prostrate, breaking wind.

Kaia pressed a thumb and finger to her nose. "But I'm only in the convent for my education. Papa will never force me to take final vows."

Her remark saddened Cathryn. She had hoped that as the only two young postulants, they might take final vows together when they were nineteen. The prospect of spending her life in the company of elderly women was depressing, especially if *Mater* Bruna was in charge. "But Javune is a monk."

"He doesn't want to be," Kaia insisted, pulling off her coif and wimple.

"*Da!*" Ekaterina repeated, filling the air with more trumpets of foul smelling wind.

Cathryn held her breath. The lone candle's flame flickered alarmingly. "What makes you think that?" she asked finally.

Kaia sighed. "He tells me with his eyes—those beautiful blue eyes."

Her words struck Cathryn like a bolt of lightning. She had noticed Javune's blue eyes, but only because colors and their many hues were important in her work. She obviously hadn't seen in his eyes what Kaia had. On the other hand it hadn't been difficult to read the dislike in Sprig's heart when he turned his dark eyes on her.

"What do you mean?" she asked hesitantly, removing her own headgear then scratching her scalp.

"He loves me," Kaia whispered, pulling her habit over her head.

"*Da!*"

Cathryn and Kaia both puffed out their cheeks, holding their breath, but no sound emerged from the dozing doyenne. When she deemed it safe to breathe again, Cathryn snorted. "How can he be in love with you? He doesn't know you, and you don't know him."

Kaia looked at her wistfully. "It was love at first sight."

Something in her friend's eyes gave her pause. She'd never seen Kaia look radiant before. "Love at first sight?" she whispered.

Kaia hunched her shoulders, beaming a smile Cathryn never suspected she had in her arsenal of facial expressions. "He makes me feel tingly." She smoothed her hands over her breasts. "Here," she whispered.

Cathryn averted her gaze from Kaia's nipples, pouting against the thin fabric of her chemise. A good nun didn't notice such things.

Then Kaia trailed a fingertip slowly down her belly to her mons. "And here," she said throatily.

Cathryn's lungs stopped working. The fetid air was suddenly too hot, the habit too confining. As her friend settled onto the second pallet, evidently lost in thoughts of Javune, she felt cast adrift from everything she had ever known. She'd grown up in the certainty she would devote her life to Saint Catherine. The martyr had been the virgin bride of Christ. Had the long dead woman she served ever tingled in those intimate places?

You are bound straight for Hell.

Certainly no one in Cathryn's life had ever made her feel that way. She clenched the inner muscles between her legs, wanting inexplicably to stretch like one of the cats that prowled the kitchens in Rouen. On the morrow she'd have to do penance for these sinful thoughts.

She quickly stripped off her habit, resisting the temptation to glance at her own strangely tingling nipples, and slumped down on the pallet next her friend.

She dozed fitfully and wasn't sure how long she'd tossed and turned when she became aware Kaia no longer slumbered beside her. She sat up abruptly, peering into the gloom. Ekaterina snored on. Kaia was gone.

Fear gripped her heart. To venture abroad at night was dangerous especially after the Abbott had mentioned there'd been reports of thieves downriver. She was certain Kaia was with Javune.

She felt around in the darkness for her habit, struggled into it and crept from the cell, fumbling with the corded belt. *Mater* had made it clear her wealthy friend was her responsibility.

TRYSTS IN THE NIGHT

Bryk had made a decision during the cross-country trek. He resented Hrolf, but the chieftain had brought them safely to Francia. His plan to coerce the King of the Franks into ceding territory made sense. The rich plains and forests they'd traversed held great promise. A man might settle here and plant apple trees, build a more comfortable and secure life than the one he'd left behind.

But the choicest lands would be doled out to those who enjoyed Hrolf's favor. Only warriors would be richly rewarded.

Bryk had courage. He didn't fear death, and would fight for a stake in this new country. But he wouldn't murder. He would win his place with honor.

He and his cohorts came to the top of a steep hill overlooking the Seine. The village of Jumièges was visible not far away and he had a good view downriver, but there was no sign of the fleet. He suspected Hrolf and the other captains had been unable to resist the temptation to raid and plunder en route.

He had come to trust the men with whom he travelled. They were inexperienced youths who'd confided that they too enjoyed the prospect of enriching themselves with booty, but assumed rape and murder went hand in hand with plundering.

Confident as he was in them, their group was too small to attack a town. His other concern was to forage for food for themselves and the horses, though there was an abundance of spring grass for grazing. Scouting the area would give him knowledge and sustenance. Hrolf would need both when he arrived.

When it was fully dark, he left his men with the wild horses, led Fisk down the steep embankment, then mounted and crossed the river. The full moon illuminated the outline of what looked like a partially finished building in the distance. It worried him; too much light made the excursion riskier.

He tied Fisk's rope to a tree and crept towards what he saw now was a stone building under construction. He remembered the tales of the sacking of the abbey at Jumièges by Vikings three score and ten years before. This edifice must be the replacement. He marveled at the perseverance of the Franks who seemed determined to rebuild with stone—a process which took much longer than the wooden construction his people used.

He suspected roofs didn't blow off stone buildings. When Hrolf gave him land, he would build with stone.

Keeping to the shadow cast by the building, he loped across to the wall and crept towards the end. He took a quick glance around the corner, expecting to see the front entryway. Instead there was only a narrow arched doorway, perhaps leading to a kitchen.

As he stepped out of the shadows, the door creaked open. He retreated quickly, flattening his body against the wall when someone came stealthily from the other side of the building.

There was enough moonlight to make out a man in robes, his head hooded. He seemed anxious not to be seen as he waited on the very spot where Bryk had stood moments earlier.

What in the name of Thor is he waiting for in the dark?

The answer came when the door creaked again and a young woman in white robes appeared. The monk pushed the hood from his head, revealing his youth, and took the girl's hands, drawing her into the shadows.

Bryk held his breath. If they detected him only paces away—

It was his understanding that men and women who had dedicated their lives to the Christian God were celibate, a notion Vikings deemed ridiculous. His young companions were apparently unaware of this obligation as they kissed ravenously, their hands wandering over each other's bodies.

A cloud crept over the moon. Bryk strained in the darkness to hear their whispers. His knowledge of the Frankish language was limited, but their clandestine endearments touched his heart and evoked cherished memories of Myldryd. He clenched his fists, guilt washing over him. Had he not turned his back on warmongering, his beautiful wife might still be alive.

The kissing couple broke apart abruptly, jolting him from his reverie. Censure in the whispered exchange that followed indicated they'd been discovered, though he'd neither seen nor heard another person approach. Annoyed with himself for his inattention, he drew his dagger and narrowed his eyes in time to see the lovers flee back around the corner of the building.

Had the unseen person left?

His breath caught in his throat when the clouds rolled on, revealing a second young woman clad in white robes. She leaned back against the wall and turned her face to the moon. She was tall and slender, and her beauty stunned him, but he swallowed hard, struck by the loneliness in her expression. He had an unwelcome urge to gather her into his arms and stroke his hand over the cropped hair that shone inky black in the moonlight.

Sensations that he'd believed long dead stirred in his loins.

Fisk nickered, catching the girl's attention. She frowned, peering into the darkness where the horse was tethered.

Alarm skittered up his spine. He willed her to return to the safety of the building, but instead she took slow, tentative steps towards his hidden mount. If she discovered the beast—

He crept up to her from behind.

When she caught sight of Fisk, she gasped and slowly offered her open palm. But then it seemed to dawn on her what the presence of the horse meant. She whirled around, her eyes filling with fear when she saw him a few paces away.

He cursed inwardly that he still held the dagger. No wonder she was terrified. She opened her mouth to scream.

Swiftly, he sheathed the weapon, snaked an arm around her back and clamped his hand over her mouth as he pulled her against him. Heat from her trembling body sparked desire, sending blood rushing to his *pikk*. But the terror in her eyes gave him pause. She thought he had rape on his mind.

"Hush," he said softly, rocking her like a baby against his chest. "Hush."

He recognized the moment her fear subsided when she went limp in his arms. Or had she fainted?

A MAN'S TOUCH

Terror rendered Cathryn incapable of movement. She swayed, certain her heart had stopped beating. It surely would when the massive barbarian plunged his knife into her breast. One glimpse of long hair, silvery blonde in the moonlight, a full beard and animal skin clothing had been enough to tell her this was no wandering peasant intent on mischief.

She had never been touched by a man. His hand was warm on her face, and it seemed he was being careful not to hurt her. At least he hadn't broken her neck. His hands were big enough to snap her like a twig. She decided in an instant biting him wasn't a good idea.

The dizzying smell of male sweat filled her nostrils, but it wasn't the acrid stink that clung to Sprig. The heat from the arm gripping her body penetrated the thick wool of her habit.

His voice was deep, but gentle. He was rocking her, which was good because her knees had buckled. Fear must have stolen her wits. How else to explain that she felt strangely safe, held firm against a male body as unyielding as a wall?

He eased her away and looked into her eyes. "No harm," he rasped.

She had lost her wits. Something in the depths of his brown eyes held her. She quickly nodded her understanding, trusting him.

He removed his hand from her mouth and they stared at each other for what seemed like long minutes.

His frown betrayed his uncertainty as to what to do with her. An urge to beg him to take her away bubbled up in her throat. She never wanted to be parted from the security of his strong arms.

But this man was a Viking—the hair, the clothing, the foreign tongue, the sheer size of him confirmed it. Women taken by Vikings became slaves.

Better a slave to this man than to Mater Bruna.

She shivered when he let go, swaying on unsteady legs until he put his hands on her waist and touched his lips to hers. The softness of his beard surprised her.

She should have been outraged, should have protested, pushed him away, called on her patron saint. But along with the alarmingly wonderful sensations coursing through her body, and a desire to have him breathe his salty breath into her, a ridiculous notion beat a tattoo in her thoughts.

Love at first sight, love at first sight.

He broke them apart, a strange look on his face, as if he too struggled to comprehend the situation in which they found themselves. He tapped his chest. "Bryk," he rasped.

Her breath caught in her dry throat but she managed to squeeze out, "Cathryn."

He smiled, sending tiny winged creatures fluttering in her lower belly.

"Cath-ryn," he repeated hoarsely.

On his lips her name was a song.

But then he put a hand on her back and pushed her gently in the direction of the abbey.

He's letting me go. I can warn the others.

She gripped his arm, unable to speak.

Don't let me go.

But he pushed her again, gesturing towards the wall. "Go," he urged, untying his horse.

She staggered away from him, crying for no good reason. Nearing the wall, she turned for one last glimpse, but he'd already disappeared, swallowed up by the night.

Loneliness shuddered through her. Blinded by tears, she resumed her walk to safety—and bumped straight into someone lurking in the shadows.

"Looking for me?" the man asked, pinning her to the wall with his body.

She'd never heard him speak but she recognized Sprig's odor. Her belly turned over at the malevolence in his voice. He spoke with an odd accent. She struggled, but he clamped his mouth on hers. She gagged on the reek of onions. He squeezed her breast. The cold stone bit into her back and fear gnawed at her gut as he forced her legs apart with his knee and yanked up her robe. His icy hand touched her thigh.

Then abruptly he was gone, crumpled in a mewling heap at her feet.

A warm hand grasped hers, and she was lifted as her legs gave way.

"Come, Cath-ryn," the Viking rumbled.

~~~

Bryk wasn't sure what made him turn back. It had been alarmingly difficult to push the woman away a second time. Visions of her lying naked beneath him on a bed of furs played behind his eyes.

It was foolish. She was a Frank, a follower of the White Christ. She'd probably raised the alarm by now. He was putting himself in harm's way—for no good reason. But he needed to be assured she was safe.

He came close to roaring his outrage when he saw what was taking place.

A man in religious garb had her up against the wall, his hand reaching under her robe, despite her protestations. In war he had witnessed many rapes and knew exactly what the man had in mind. Evidently nothing he'd been told about Christian clerics was true.

Intent on his evil deed, her attacker apparently didn't hear Bryk steal up behind him. A swift chop to the base of his skull dropped him like a stone.

Thanks be to Freyja he'd returned in time. Cath-ryn stared at him, shaking uncontrollably, seemingly on the verge of hysteria. He couldn't walk away. Her attacker's moans indicated he wasn't dead. He would likely try for her again, or exact revenge. Taking her with him would cause difficulties. He had nothing to offer but the life of a thrall.

This young woman drew him like a lodestone. And how was it he had changed in the blink of an eye from a man who'd forsworn murder to one resolved to kill anyone who touched her? Perhaps she was a witch who'd put a *heks* on him. He had no choice.

"*Kom*! Cath-ryn," he said urgently as he scooped her up and carried her to his horse.

A VIKING'S CAPTIVE

Cathryn had never ridden, but she liked being cradled in the Viking's arms. However, worry gnawed at her. "The alarm will be raised," she told him.

He seemed to understand. "*Ja*. Alarm."

But they rode on.

She prayed Javune and Kaia were safe.

Was Sprig dead? She shivered, recalling the paralyzing terror when she feared the odious monk would succeed in raping her. It was strange how one man's touch was thrilling and another's repellent.

They reached the river and the horse readily waded into the dark water. Cathryn had lived her life in a convent overlooking this same river, but had never been allowed to venture near it, until the voyage aboard the *Bonvent*. Fear took hold. She snaked her arms around her captor's neck. He tightened his grip. "Safe," he whispered in her ear.

His warm breath and calm demeanor reassured her. They reached the opposite bank and scaled an embankment. His arms stiffened. A small group of similarly clad men surrounded them as they rode into a glade. She should have known he wouldn't be alone. Vikings always came in hordes.

He said something to the men in his language, his voice stern. They looked from him to her. What lurked in their eyes? Disbelief, resentment? Certainly not welcome.

~~~

41

"This woman is my captive," Bryk declared, knowing his cohorts would understand completely. To make sure, he added, "I claim her as my thrall."

Without a word they drifted away to the shelter of the trees.

He dismounted, then pulled Cath-ryn into his arms, relieved she had stopped shaking. But he recognized the fear and uncertainty in her eyes and he wanted it gone. "Safe," he repeated, wishing he knew more of her tongue.

She replied in her own language. She was perhaps uttering her thanks, and he was elated when she timidly took his hand and added, "*Takk*."

She speaks my language!

"It was nothing," he replied hastily, wanting to warm her chilled hand. "I couldn't let him—"

But it was evident from her frown he'd spoken too quickly. He barely understood his actions. How to explain them to her? She was here and now he would have to take care of her. He'd always seen to the welfare of his thralls, clothed and fed and sheltered them. But strangely the prospect of this woman as his thrall didn't appeal. Not that she wasn't desirable, despite the ugly robe. The persistent hardening of the flesh between his legs that he'd tried unsuccessfully to will away was proof of it.

It was his right to take her, willing or not, if she were his slave. But the prospect of taking her by force filled him with dismay.

The stirrings were welcome, if inconvenient. He thought his interest in women had died with Myldryd.

He raked a hand through his hair, worried there might be pursuit from the abbey. She watched then pointed to her head. She said a word in her language, and he repeated it. "Hair."

She smiled. "Good."

He laughed, assuming he'd said it correctly. He reached out and sifted his fingers through her black hair, repeating the word, then trailed his fingertips down her neck. Her face darkened as she moved away, putting both hands on her head.

He understood. Women in Norway never went about with their hair uncovered. She obviously hadn't expected to come across a Viking in the middle of the night. He chuckled, wishing his belongings weren't on board the *Seahorse*.

Her eyes widened in alarm when he took out his dagger. He feared she might swoon when he untied the leather belt of his *kyrtill* and tugged it over his head. It was chilly without the woolen overtunic. He quickly peeled off his linen shirt and sliced through the hem of braided wool then tore off a piece of the long garment he judged ample for a scarf.

He handed her the fabric and patted the top of his head. She stared wide-eyed at his chest and it occurred to him suddenly she had probably never seen a half naked man before. As a warrior he'd trained long and hard to keep fit. Farming had kept his muscles strong, his body lean. He had a momentary notion to strut like a rooster, but thought better of it. He quickly redonned his shirt and *kyrtill*, welcoming the protection when his thighs were again covered by the woolen garment. He hoped she'd been unaware of the significance of the bulge at his groin.

She finally seemed to understand his intent, covered her head with the fabric and knotted it under her chin. The ripped edging Myldryd had lovingly braided framed her face.

~~~

Bryk settled Cathryn into a hollow at the base of a tree. Horses whinnied and snorted nearby. He motioned for her to stay where she was then strode off on long legs in the direction of the men.

She was afraid she might be sick. The trembling had begun again. She wished he hadn't left her alone. In the space of a few minutes she'd gone from terror, believing Bryk intended to rape and kill her, to salivating at the site of steam rising from his bared body in the chilly night air, the moonlight glowing silver on metal bands around his upper arms.

She ought to have known he would do her no harm. He'd understood her alarm at realizing her hair was uncovered and sacrificed part of his own garment to fashion a scarf.

As she fingered the knot under her chin, she had a fanciful urge to toss the fabric away, to beg him to run his fingers through her hair again. Her scalp had tingled beneath his gentle touch. She traced a fingertip down her neck, aware for the first time how sensitive her skin was. The prospect of putting back on the coif she'd worn since childhood suddenly lodged in her belly like a lead weight.

His hair was as blond as hers was dark, and long where hers was short, cropped for comfort under the coif and wimple. But the gleam in his eye told her he liked it.

Perhaps now she was free, her hair would grow.

Free?

Instead of being preoccupied with meaningless trivialities she should worry he might sell or enslave her. Staying with these men wouldn't mean freedom. She'd never been at liberty to come and go as she wished. The life she'd accepted as her destiny suddenly rankled. It didn't make sense.

What did these Vikings intend? What was Bryk doing lurking near the abbey? It was obvious they intended to attack. The monks and nuns there would be slaughtered. Brother Javune. Kaia.

She struggled to her feet as Bryk approached, his men close behind, their jaws clenched. Some decision had been reached; she saw it on his face and the axe in his grip confirmed what she dreaded. He took her hand. "Jumièges," he said as he pulled her in the direction of his horse.

STAMPEDE

Bryk was depending heavily on a hunch there would be no armed Frankish soldiers in the vicinity of the abbey. And how many monks could there be in a partially finished building? There'd be few stonemasons at work before dawn.

However, if the foul smelling monk had raised the alarm, the local peasantry would quickly arm itself and come looking for the enemy.

He had no choice but to take the fight to them and hope intimidation and terror would make up for the size of his raiding party.

Cath-ryn resisted when he pulled her towards his horse. He turned to her, filled with regret for the fear he had once again brought to her lovely face. But she would eventually see he wasn't a murdering barbarian. Why her opinion mattered he wasn't sure. "I cannot leave you here," he rasped, growling and licking his lips like a hungry predator. "Wolves."

He howled at the moon to make sure she understood.

Nervously, she looked into the shadows, then came willingly.

She gripped his shoulders when he put his hands on her waist to lift her onto Fisk. It was like lifting a feather. He searched for some way to reassure this delicate female. It was risky, but he drew his dagger, rested it on his palm and offered it, hilt first.

She looked at the weapon, then at him, her eyes wide.

The Viking his grandfather had carved into the ivory handle stood out in sharp relief in the moonlight.

"Take," he said sternly, wondering if it was wise to give away his talisman. "Protect."

She took hold of the handle with trembling hands paler than the ivory, but didn't drop it as he feared she might. Instead she stared at it.

Was she contemplating plunging it into his back? The uncertainty in her eyes when she finally looked at him calmed his fears. She simply didn't know what to do with it.

His men moved restlessly, their faces anxious. They were youths, looking to him as the seasoned warrior to lead them in what was likely their first raid.

He quickly grasped her hand and wound the tasseled end of her corded belt around the blade then tucked it in at her hip. "Careful," he whispered with a wink.

She smiled weakly, her palm flattened over the weapon.

He mounted Fisk in front of her, elated when she clamped her arms around his waist and pressed her breasts to his back. She likely had no idea of the effect she was having on his manhood.

This had to be the strangest Viking raid in the glorious history of his people; a farmer and a nun leading a raiding party consisting of a handful of youths and a few wild horses.

For reassurance he looked to the sky and mumbled. "Lend us your aid, mighty Thor, god of war."

"Thor," Cath-ryn whispered into his back, followed by something that sounded like her own name.

~~~

As the water lapped around the horse's legs, Cathryn repeated her prayer for deliverance to her namesake saint over and over like a litany. But they'd traveled only a few yards on the opposite bank when she saw her entreaties to Saint Catherine had been for naught. She chided herself. It had been naive to assume the alarm wouldn't have been raised.

Panicked voices reached her ears and in the pre-dawn darkness the abbey was lit by the glow of torches. Bryk dismounted and lifted her down. Despite the rapid beating of her heart, the strength of his big hands calmed her roiling belly.

He motioned to the men to remain with the horses, then took her hand and crept forward. At the edge of the trees they stopped and crouched down.

Mater Bruna will be livid that I've soiled my habit!

She almost laughed out loud at the absurdity of her thoughts. It was unlikely she'd live long enough to see the mean-spirited Superior again. At least the last hours of her existence would be filled with life.

Her brawny Viking had made her feel more alive than ever before.

The crowd was boisterous, peasants mostly and a few monks. She narrowed her eyes, trying to make out faces. She recognized the tall man calmly issuing orders to the monks. "Father Abbot," she whispered, turning to Bryk. "Please don't kill him."

He nodded. *"Fader."*

Had he understood?

Then she spied Javune carrying a torch and murmured his name.

Bryk chuckled, making the shape of a woman with his hands and kissing sounds with his lips. She knew then he'd seen the young monk with Kaia.

She was about to return his smile when her attacker strode into view, gesturing wildly and shouting loudly. Bile rose in her throat and for the first time in her life she felt hatred for another person. "Sprig," she said hoarsely, gripping the handle of the dagger.

Bryk shifted his weight, his teeth gritted. "Spreeg," he spat, brandishing his axe. "I kill."

Much as she might want the monk punished, she couldn't condone murder. "No," she whispered, pushing down his raised arm. "God will punish."

He looked at her strangely, his eyes wide. She might drown in those dark brown depths. She recognised now what Kaia had seen in Javune's eyes.

But no! Kaia had seen love. She wasn't sure what she saw in Bryk's eyes, and this was not the time to be thinking such thoughts.

There was no sign of her friend nor of Ekaterina. The elderly nun must be terrified. There'd be scant air for Kaia to breathe if both women were closeted in the tiny cell.

The peasants had armed themselves with pitchforks and sickles.

As the first grey steaks of dawn lit the sky, Bryk put a hand on her shoulder. "Stay," he ordered, and then crept back to his men.

Close to panic at being left alone, she was startled by loud shouts behind her. Moments later she curled into a ball and covered her ears as wild horses stampeded past in the direction of the abbey.

~~~

Among the many things Bryk had learned during his years as a plundering marauder, probably the most important was the effective use of surprise.

If a raider didn't hold the advantage, he had to be bold and make his enemy believe he did. He'd hoped that if they made enough noise and panicked the wild horses, the armed mob might assume a Viking horde was attacking when the beasts arrived in their midst.

He knew from experience there was nothing like horses running amok to make grown men wet themselves.

As he had foreseen, the villagers dispersed rapidly when the frenzied animals galloped out of the trees. Most dropped their tools as they fled. One or two waved their arms in an effort to turn the beasts, but quickly abandoned the idea when Bryk and his men emerged from the forest. He had instructed his band to yell with gusto and brandish their weapons menacingly, but only those who posed a genuine threat were to be rendered harmless or killed.

By the time the sun was up, they had ten monks lined up with their backs to the abbey wall, a score of villagers and workmen roped together, and two nuns tending to the handful of wounded. One of the nuns was the girl of the tryst. The other was ancient.

As his men corralled the last of the horses, he strode over to the monks. To his surprise the old nun followed him. She beamed a big smile, took hold of his hand and addressed him in his language. "I am Sister Ekaterina. In the name of God, and our beloved Saint Catherine of Alexandria, we welcome you, Viking." She pointed to the axe in his other hand. "You could have killed us all, but you chose not to."

His astonishment grew when she spoke to the man he recognized as the Abbot, pointing and gesturing, evidently repeating what she had said to him. The elderly monk seemed to have difficulty understanding her, but she persevered and he eventually made a sign over Bryk with his hand. It was one Christians made as a blessing and he returned the captive's nod.

The monk who had attacked Cath-ryn stepped forward, his face a mask of hatred. "What have you done with the nun, barbarian?"

Ekaterina scowled at the monk as she translated.

Bryk grabbed the front of the man's robes with his free hand and dragged him to his knees. "She is safe, no thanks to you." He looked to the Abbot. "This man called Spreeg attacked Cath-ryn."

Disbelief spread on the Abbot's face as Ekaterina explained.

Sprig scrambled to his feet. "You believe the lies of a barbarian? I am a monk. I have dedicated my life to God. He has stolen Cathryn away."

"But he knows your name, my son, how can that be?" the Abbot asked, his voice gentle.

Sweat broke out on Spreeg's forehead. "He must have tortured her. Perhaps she called out for my help."

Bryk had an urge to lop off the man's head and be done with the matter, but he remembered Cath-ryn staying his hand. He didn't see her approach from the trees, but there was no mistaking the joy on Ekaterina's face as she waddled past him.

"*Da!* My child," she gushed.

He turned to see her fold Cath-ryn in a warm embrace. She kissed Ekaterina's forehead then faced Spreeg. "The Viking speaks true, my lord Abbot. I believe Brother Sprig would have violated me if the Viking hadn't come to my rescue."

It irritated Bryk that Cath-ryn didn't call him by name. "My name is Bryk Gardbruker," he told the Abbot. "Cath-ryn knows this and I speak the truth."

When the elderly nun repeated what he'd said it prompted an exchange of rapid glances between her and the Abbot.

Cath-ryn blushed and seemed reluctant to look at him.

He'd evidently said something to embarrass her.

Ekatarina grinned like a child as if she were privy to the world's biggest secret. "*Da!*" she exclaimed.

THE LIBRARY

Two days later Cathryn strained without success to catch a glimpse of the river through the narrow window slit in the library, surely designed to make sure monks weren't distracted by anything going on outside.

One of Bryk's men stationed downriver had sighted longboats approaching. He had immediately ordered the women into the library, and consigned the monks to their cells. The workmen were sent back to the village and instructed to remain there.

His apprehension at the arrival of the man he called his chieftain was evident. Would the Viking leader show the same restraint or would they be massacred?

Cathryn marveled how in two days Bryk had taken full control of Jumièges with a handful of men. Only two villagers had been killed during the raid, for which the local inhabitants were grateful. Everyone was aware of the atrocities perpetrated when the Vikings had last come to Jumièges. More than one thousand monks had been slaughtered, the abbey sacked.

Bryk was a man who commanded respect. He had shown mercy to Sprig, listening to the Abbot's suggestion that the monk be confined to his cell.

He questioned the stonemasons about the construction of the abbey, inspected the cottages in the village, tallied the town's provisions. Ekaterina went with him. Cathryn did not.

He seemed anxious to avoid her. She longed for another kiss, for his touch, for any sign he cared. At night she clutched the scarf to her breast, tracing her fingertip along the intricate braiding on one edge, inhaling his scent. She'd never set eyes on the sea but she rode the waves with him when she licked the salt from the fibers. In two days she had turned into a seething mess of thwarted wantonness, jealous of an ancient nun because Bryk fussed over her.

It was foolish. Soon he would be gone. She was being tested.

She pulled away from the window. "I suppose now his people are coming, he will leave," she said to Ekaterina. "They will plunder and destroy, then return to their native land."

"*Nyet*," came the unexpected reply. "They settle in Francia."

Her heart did a peculiar somersault. "Settle? King Charles won't permit it."

Ekaterina shrugged, smiling one of her enigmatic smiles. "Don't *vorry*," she whispered.

Kaia sauntered over to the window slit. "I can't see anything," she said, her voice flat. She'd been pouting for two days because she'd seen nothing of Javune. Cathryn wondered if her own preoccupation with Bryk was as obvious.

"Gardbruker," Ekaterina said.

Had the old woman read her mind? "What?"

"His last name means he is a farmer."

Cathryn came close to snorting. "Farmer?"

"*Da*. He *vants* to cultivate apple orchards in Francia."

Cathryn didn't know what to make of this startling revelation. Her thoughts went to the river where the gentle farmer was greeting his warrior chieftain.

Watch over him, Saint Catherine.

~~~

Stroking the pad of his thumb over the carved Viking on the handle of his dagger, Bryk kept his eyes on Hrolf as the chieftain brought his longboat to shore. Cath-ryn had returned the talisman to him. He hoped she would have no further need of a weapon when Hrolf took over the town.

Many of the boats rode lower in the water. His countrymen had indeed stopped along the way to help themselves to treasures which now lay no doubt in the men's sea chests.

He gritted his teeth when he noticed Alfred was missing. But it wouldn't be wise to let his alarm show.

He relished the prospect of explaining how he had captured Jumièges with a handful of inexperienced men and precious little blood spilled. It would raise his standing, allowing him to protect the woman he'd taken.

He wasn't sure why he was preoccupied with her. She was a Christian who had dedicated her life to the *Vite Krist*. His thoughts wandered to the brief kiss they'd shared. Her sweet taste had taken him off guard. She hadn't fought him like she'd fought the monk. Indeed, it was as if she'd enjoyed it— thoroughly. And certainly he had. Perhaps next time he might delve his tongue—

His musings were interrupted when Hrolf jumped from the boat and strode over to him. "Gardbruker."

He bowed slightly, satisfied that the sloping bank allowed him to look the giant in the eye. He hoped the carnal heat spreading through his body wasn't evident on his face. Better to get his mind off tongues mating. "It is safe to let everyone come ashore. I have secured the town."

Hrolf frowned, looking to the buildings beyond. "Secured?"

Bryk quickly summarized events, then paused before making his last remark. "I deemed it wise to kill as few men as possible. If we wish to ultimately be welcomed here, we should show that we are civilized people with much to offer."

Hrolf stared at him for long minutes until Vilhelm came up the bank. Bryk took advantage of the moment. "You want your son to rule here in peace, do you not?"

Hrolf clamped a hand on his son's shoulder and grinned. "Indeed. Lead on Bryk *Kriger*. Let us see this town you have captured single handedly."

Bryk was still a farmer at heart, but was elated Hrolf had recognized him as a warrior. Part of it was because he'd appealed to Hrolf's vanity, having guessed the chieftain harbored visions of establishing a ruling dynasty. However, he'd proven a man didn't need to be a bloodthirsty savage to be a warrior. "My brother? Alfred?" he asked.

"Coming overland with captives and livestock. Too many— they'd have swamped a boat. Besides we needed room for the pig."

It was then Bryk noticed the hubbub on board the *Seahorse*. The crewmen were attempting to land a very pregnant sow that looked ready to drop a litter at any moment.

Laughing, Hrolf gave the command for his people to come ashore, then turned to his son. "Fetch your mother. I want her to accompany me as we walk abroad in our new land."

Bryk waited, watching the enraged pig intimidate burly warriors who had no idea how to handle her. Alfred was probably happy to be on dry land, but he'd have known how to calm the sow.

~~~

Ekaterina had dozed off in a library chair.

In an effort to calm her frayed nerves, Cathryn mixed paint and resumed work on a partially finished illumination. It was one Sprig had begun and would need her full concentration if she was to correct his careless work.

She tried to ignore Kaia's nervous pacing and the din drifting in from outside. Evidently the Viking chieftain had arrived with a horde. She was surprised to hear the excited voices of children. The raiders had brought their families. Perhaps it was true they intended to settle in Francia. Did Bryk have a wife and children?

She had no trouble picturing him with his own brood. He was a gentle giant. She remembered the night they had met, when he'd—

"They're coming," Kaia hissed, hurrying away from the wooden door as it was thrust open.

Ekaterina woke with a snort accompanied by another sound Cathryn recognized.

She came to her feet too quickly, tipping her stool. It clattered to the planked floor. Dropping her quill added to her confusion.

Bryk was the biggest man she had ever seen, until a bearded giant strode into the library. The smell of leather and the sea overpowered even the unpleasant odor of flatulence. The woman with him seemed tiny in comparison, yet there was something striking about her—a nobility, evident despite her wrinkled nose. Her eyes darted here and there, perhaps searching out the culprit who'd fouled the air.

Bryk and a boy followed the pair. Was this his son?

To her surprise it was the woman who spoke first. "I am Poppa, wife to Hrolf Ganger," she said in the Frankish tongue, indicating the giant. "Vilhelm is our son."

Relief swept over her—the boy wasn't the child of her Viking. She ought to have known by the resemblance wrought by the similarly wrinkled noses. But this woman spoke her language.

"I am the daughter of Berengar, Count of Bayeux," the woman continued. "My husband killed my father and destroyed my home many years ago during a raid on our town. He took me to Norway, where I have lived ever since."

This didn't sound right. Vikings never married their captives. They enslaved them. The still silent Hrolf must have prized this woman.

She glanced at him, perturbed to see he was staring at her, unmistakable lust in his gaze. Fear skittered up her spine.

Bryk strode to where she stood and took her hand. He said something that caused Hrolf to scowl.

The woman smiled. "Bryk says you are his captive, under his protection." She shot a gloating glance at her husband who finally spoke after clearing his throat. It seemed the woman had the upper hand in their relationship, but there was no doubt Hrolf was used to being obeyed.

"He says you have nothing to fear," Poppa explained. "We come in peace, seeking a new land."

"*Da!*" Ekaterina said with great conviction and to the surprise of everyone.

Buoyed by the strength of Bryk's hand, Cathryn found her voice. "But King Charles will oppose you."

Hrolf replied immediately. "We are not afraid to fight for a piece of this land."

"You speak my language," she blurted out.

Hrolf chuckled. "I visited Francia many years ago, and claimed my lovely Poppa. She has taught me."

Poppa wandered over to the workbench, examining the vellum Cathryn had been working on. "You are illuminating? It's a rare skill, especially for a woman."

Cathryn glanced up at Bryk. He had tightened his grip on her hand and was staring at her work, admiration in his eyes. "You?" he asked.

She wished the sample was one of her own better pieces. "It's for the altar bible."

"Beautiful," he breathed in her language. The word rolled off his foreign tongue, sending shards of longing scurrying up her thighs.

"She's a nun, Bryk," Poppa said, first in his language then in Cathryn's. "Married to the White Christ. I am still a Christian. Do not offend me by lusting after her."

"But I'm not a nun," Cathryn said hastily. "I haven't taken my final vows, or any vows for that matter. I was a foundling left at the door of the abbey."

Poppa stared first at her then at Bryk. "Where are you from, which convent?"

"Saint Catherine of Alexandria, in Rouen."

"Aha! Rouen!" Hrolf shouted, startling everyone. "Our next port of call."

THE INVINCIBLE BARBARIAN

E katerina perched atop an iron chest on board the *Seahorse*, her smiling face turned to the wind, booted feet planted firmly on the deck. Her gnarled and mottled hands gripped the smooth metal. Occasionally, she called out *Splash, Splash* in cadence with the rhythm of the oars. The men pulling those oars chuckled each time, to which she dutifully responded, "*Da!*"

For Cathryn, riding in a longboat was different from sailing aboard the *Bonvent*. It was smaller than the trading ship, but she felt safer. However, she too held firmly to the bronze-clad sides of the sturdy wooden sea chest Bryk had given her to sit on. Her pigments and quills were tucked inside, along with the axe she remembered from the night of their meeting.

Kaia offered no conversation. She had sulked and sobbed alternately since leaving Javune in Jumièges.

Hrolf and his son stood at the prow. Cathryn had her back to them, but sensed the Viking leader's excitement as they drew closer to Rouen. Her own heart skittered around in her chest— life had changed considerably in the short time since she'd left the town of her birth.

She studied the scenery, trying not to let her eyes wander to Bryk, who held firm to the tiller at the rear of the vessel.

The task of keeping the heavy boat steady in the winding river seemed effortless for him. He wore a knee-length shaggy cloak the color and texture of sheepskin, pushed back off his shoulders to reveal a faded red lining. It was fastened at the shoulder with a pin held captive in an elaborately decorated gold circle. A woolen braid similar to the one on her scarf edged the cloak. Someone had fashioned the well used garment with love.

A crimson shirt had replaced the one he'd torn apart. Tight pants clung to his muscular thighs, a narrow leather belt snaking its way through the loops at his waist. A large pouch made of some animal skin hung from it. She suspected the key to the iron padlock that secured the chest lay inside. The buckle was ornate, silver perhaps. An enormous sword sat on his hip that she would have difficulty lifting. She recognized the hilt of a familiar dagger tucked within easy reach.

A cow horn etched with what looked like a two-headed ship hung from a lanyard suspended across his body. Perhaps he used it for drinking.

His shins were wrapped in strips of braided fabric which disappeared inside calf high leather boots fastened with toggles.

Perched atop his head was a rounded helmet with chain mail hanging from it to protect his neck. Metal flaps covered his ears. But the studded metal mask encircling his eyes and covering his nose were the most menacing aspect. A zigzag pattern had been hammered into it, the oval eye slits transforming him into a creature of myth, a bird-like raptor. She was relieved he hadn't worn it the night they'd met. She'd have died of fright.

He was the embodiment of every tale she'd ever heard about Vikings—a battle-ready barbarian. The helmet must weigh a considerable amount, yet he showed no sign of discomfort.

She squirmed on the chest, clenching pulsating inner muscles she never knew she had, aware his heavy outer tunic was within, as well as his armor.

He was a man who sailed the perilous seas. He had shaved his beard, though not closely. Stubble still shadowed his rugged features. Had the wind and sun turned his hair to gold as they had bronzed his face and arms? Was his chest the same burnished hue? It had been impossible to tell when he'd stripped off his shirt in the darkness and she'd been too awe-struck at the size of him. Could she mix paint from her pigments to match?

She studied him, painting a picture behind her eyes, looking away quickly when she became aware he was staring back, a strange smile on his chiseled face. Had he guessed her lustful longing to be the woman such a man clung to in the night?

She was damned.

Saint Catherine intercede for me. I am losing my wits.

She fretted over why he had insisted to Hrolf she be brought along, though she was glad of it. She understood Ekaterina's value as a translator, but a battle loomed. And why were they in a boat with the men and not with the women? They would have been safer in Jumièges. Except Sprig was still there.

~~~

Bryk thanked the gods for his good fortune. Not only had Hrolf acceded to his demands he bring Cath-ryn, he'd promoted him to navigator. It was important his captive not think him an oarsman.

He'd not wanted to leave her in Jumièges. The fifty Vikings who held the town would surely keep Sprig confined, but he felt a keen need to be her protector.

It was absurd. He was taking her into a siege to keep her safe. But most of the men who'd made the journey from Møre faced the same dilemma. He had a better understanding of Alfred's anxieties for his family.

He pushed his cloak further back off his shoulders, studying the river's unpredictable flow. Navigating these waters required more concentration than gliding up a fjord. He had to admit it was good to be back in action. Working the land was satisfying, but there was much to be said for a sturdy ship beneath a man's feet and the prospect of battle ahead.

He recalled something Hrolf often repeated. *"It is better to live on the sea and let others raise your crops and cook your meals. A house smells of smoke, a ship smells of frolic. From a house you see a sooty roof, from a ship you see Valhalla."*

He hazarded a glance at Cath-ryn. She looked away quickly. Perhaps she would be the one to fill his house with the tempting aromas of her cooking. She sat atop his sea chest, as if she was already his—

The word he'd conjured gave him pause. He didn't want another wife. A foreign captive could not marry a Viking. Hrolf had never wed his Frankish concubine, only pledging to her *more danico*. Cath-ryn was his possession, like the sea chest.

He wondered what she thought of his war helmet and hoped he didn't look too menacing. He laughed out loud at the ridiculousness of the notion—the helmet was meant to give the impression he was an invincible barbarian.

He had secured clothing for her from Poppa. Asking Alfred's wife would have caused hardship. The voluminous white robe of the Christian God was badly soiled and the ugly headgear that hid most of her lovely face irritated him. His chieftain's concubine had balked at first, insinuating that Cath-ryn was probably unaware of the ways of Vikings.

But Hrolf had supported his insistence she couldn't remain in the religious community. She'd implied as much. She was his thrall, and from the glint in her eye and the way she gazed at him, he was confident she was a woman born to share a man's bed. These errant thoughts produced a pleasant but inconvenient stiffening at his groin. It was unfortunate his long *kyrtill* was in his chest. But the weather had warmed and he'd have been too hot if he'd worn it at the tiller. However, he was assured the pouch hid his arousal. It held a few coins brought from home and of no practical use. There was a scrap of clean cloth to wipe his hands and face, a fire starting kit, a whetstone, and a lock of Myldryd's hair, braided into a circle—and the key to his chest.

There was also a key to the farmhouse in Møre—a keepsake.

He feared the woolen under-dress Poppa had provided for Cath-ryn might be overly heavy. She appeared comfortable though it was tight around the breasts. The robe had hidden the bounty of her perfect globes. He mused about the color of her nipples, probably dark, given her black hair, then wished he'd avoided the notion as his arousal surged.

He shifted his gaze to the cup-shaped silver brooches holding up the straps of her *hangerock*, the linen over-dress Poppa's thrall had helped her fasten. The brooches were a generous gift, but they looked too much like breasts for his comfort. Funny he'd never noticed it before though all the wealthier women wore them.

"Too well dressed for a thrall," Poppa had mumbled when they'd emerged from the curtained off area reserved for females. His heart had filled with contentment. She looked like a Viking noblewoman—except she'd evidently declined the offer of a traditional headdress, opting instead for his scarf, which fluttered in the breeze.

Hrolf's concubine had never fully accepted her role as a captive, but he suspected she loved Hrolf. There was no doubt in his mind the chieftain loved her.

But would Cath-ryn accept being a thrall? In his confused mind he couldn't think of her as one of his slaves. They were well taken care of, but he didn't love them.

Love?

As another swift bend in the meandering river appeared ahead, he wondered if he had made a mistake in claiming his prize.

His gaze chanced upon Ekaterina, who was staring at him, shaking her head.

SACRED VESTMENTS

Cathryn reluctantly twisted around to face the town where she'd lived all her life. It seemed eerily quiet. No doubt the alarm had been raised, prompting citizens in the low-lying areas to flee. She raised her gaze beyond the cathedral to the distant hill where the abbey convent stood. Many would be sheltering there.

She turned away.

As if sensing her turmoil, Bryk shaded his eyes and looked to the hill.

Hrolf ordered the longboats to pull in at the island where the chapel of Saint-Éloi stood. "First stop," he declared.

Without another word from their leader, hundreds of men swarmed off the boats. Bryk handed the tiller over to another seaman after everyone else had left. He took off his cloak and draped it over her shoulders. He donned the mailshirt from his chest, tucked the axe into his belt, then put a hand on her shoulder. "Stay. Short time."

No use begging him not to go, not to leave her. What would happen to her if he failed to return? She buried her nose in the cloak, inhaling his comforting scent.

Ekaterina waddled over to her. "All shall be well," she crooned.

More than a hundred longboats sat at anchor and shorebirds danced on the wind, calling raucously, yet the silence seemed overwhelming. Cathryn could barely make out the boats with the women at the end of the line, but sensed they too were praying to their gods for the safe return of the men.

It occurred to her that this was an opportunity to flee. The lone sailor wouldn't leave his post on the boat. Judging by the shouts of elation coming from the church, the Vikings were busy gathering whatever there was of value. If she and Kaia leapt into the shallow water—

But it would be impossible to take Ekaterina. Several islands dotted the Seine, each with a church of its own—Saint-Clément, Saint-Stephen. How to get from one to the other and then through the deserted town itself?

In her heart she didn't want to leave because Bryk had asked her to stay.

~~~

Once Hrolf had claimed whatever treasures the priests hadn't carried off, there wasn't much else of value in the little chapel. Bryk was relieved no one had remained to defend the edifice. As his grumbling comrades trooped out to ransack the few hovels on the island and then muster for the next church, he cast about for some keepsake. He knew from long experience where a patient raider might discover hidden treasures.

He crouched down beside the stone altar and put his shoulder to it. It moved an inch or two away from the wall. He braced his legs and pushed again, this time making a space barely wide enough for his arm.

He snaked a hand up underneath the stone lip. As he'd suspected, there was a hidden shelf. His fingers touched fabric. He dragged out the bundle—vestments, folded and crammed into the hidey-hole. He danced his fingers along the shelf again, discovering several good sized candle ends, one of which was still wedged on a pointed gold candlestick.

He understood some cleric taking time to conceal the candlestick and the vestments, but risking one's life for spent candle ends?

Alfred's wife could use the heavy fabric, and perhaps Cath-ryn would like the gold braiding and the candlestick.

By Thor, this preoccupation has to stop.

He'd asked Alfred to keep an eye on her when he'd handed over the tiller. His brother might not be a warrior, but he would defend Bryk's property. As he made his way back to the boat, his heart reassured him she wouldn't try to flee.

Nevertheless, he let out a long slow breath when he caught sight of her, still sitting on his chest, as if guarding it. She scowled at the men stowing their meager treasures.

Her eyes betrayed her happiness at his return when she saw him. It felt good that someone cared whether he lived or died. He motioned for her to rise, lifted the lid of his chest and threw in the candle remnants. He'd show her the candlestick later, when they weren't surrounded by fifty pairs of greedy eyes. As he stuffed in the vestments, he had an inkling there was something wrapped inside—also for later.

He had to sit on the lid to close the chest. Cath-ryn quickly lost the scowl that had crossed her face on seeing the vestments and sat next to him, laughing, wriggling to add weight to the effort. Raiding had never been this enjoyable.

He pointed to the chest, then pulled at his *kyrtill*. "Alfred," he said, cocking his head towards the tiller. "*Bror.*" He held up ten fingers. "*Barn.* Chilrens."

Wide-eyed, she glanced over to Alfred, touching her fingers to his as she counted. "He's your brother and he has ten children?"

The contact between them was light as air, yet her warmth seeped into him. Her delicate white hands and slender fingers made his look weathered and stained. "*Ja.*"

She frowned, moving a fingertip to his chest. "How many children do you have?"

The painful memories hit him like the heel of a *stridsøkse*.

"No lamb for the lazy wolf," Hrolf shouted from the prow. "To oars. Clement's church awaits."

Rescued from his torment, Bryk breathed again as he made his way back to the tiller, his thoughts unexpectedly filling with an image of a child born of a black haired woman and a fair-haired man.

ROUEN FALLS

In the darkness Cathryn and Kaia huddled together on the sea chest, Bryk's cloak around their shoulders. Ekaterina lay in the bottom of the gently rocking longboat, snoring loudly, seemingly oblivious to the damp cold. Cathryn thought of taking out the priestly vestments and spreading them over the elderly nun, but the chest was locked, and *La Russe* might consider it a sacrilege.

She was happy to be free of the white habit the other women still wore. How Ekaterina managed to keep hers spotless was a mystery.

The sun had set hours before, long after the Vikings had gone ashore to plunder the main part of the town, including the cathedral. At first, shouts and screams had drifted to their ears, but now everything had fallen quiet, the only sound the lapping of the black water against the boats. Smoke from earlier fires hung in the still air.

They hadn't eaten since Bryk had brought bread and cheese after the raid on Saint-Clément.

But Cathryn's greater hunger was to see Bryk return safely. She searched her heart for the reason he had become important to her in only a few days. To never see him again would be a worse torment than anything Saint Catherine had ever suffered.

It was a blasphemous thought.

Hearing footsteps, she peered nervously into the darkness. Poppa emerged from the gloom, accompanied by several women all chattering happily. She climbed into the *Seahorse.* "They have taken the town," she said softly.

Cathryn supposed she should stand to greet the chieftain's wife, but she was too cold, her limbs stiff. She looked towards the cathedral. "I don't understand."

"Listen."

Off in the distance, she thought she heard—

Ekaterina's eyes blinked open. "*Zinging,*" she said with her usual smile.

Poppa laughed. "Prepare yourselves. They will return for us shortly."

Cathryn felt like an old woman as she and Kaia came to their feet then pulled Ekaterina up from the deck. They clung together trying to keep their balance in the rocking boat, sharing the cloak. Poppa seemed to have no such difficulty. She climbed out gracefully, rejoined her companions and disappeared into the darkness.

The sound of male voices raised in song became louder. Soon men were on board, many of them reeling from drink, all with smoke-smudged faces, some bloodied. They set about stuffing objects into their chests. The boat rocked alarmingly as en masse they climbed over the rail, the chests on their shoulders, headed in the direction of the women's boats.

A lump refused to dislodge itself from Cathryn's throat. Bryk and Hrolf had not returned.

~~~

"You were right, my friend," Hrolf rasped between hiccups, leaning heavily against Bryk.

He tightened his grip on his chieftain's waist, keeping him upright lest he fall face first in the muck as they staggered towards the *Seahorse.*

When they'd left Møre he was a social outcast; now he was Hrolf's *friend.* His advice had been true. "There is no need for slaughter. Dispatch only those who offer armed resistance. We will need people alive to work the land when it is ours," he'd told his leader.

And Hrolf had listened.

Now they controlled the town, though they'd encountered scant numbers of terrified peasants, monks and priests, but no Frankish soldiers, and no-one of importance. He had a suspicion many had sought refuge in Cath-ryn's convent, but he kept this notion to himself. Once people came to see they had little to fear from the rule of Vikings, they would emerge and return to the town.

He'd taken no plunder. Land was what he wanted, and his chest was already over full. He'd have to throw out some of his rootstocks to make room and he had no intention of doing that.

Nor had he imbibed any of the freely flowing wine and ale, not wanting Cath-ryn to think him a drunken barbarian. She'd been in his thoughts throughout the attack. Rouen was where she lived. He understood why she had scant knowledge of the place, but how did his involvement in the sacking of her town affect her, and why by all the gods did it matter to him?

He'd anticipated seeing her again, but his elation when he set eyes on her in the darkness had him tempted to let his drunken chieftain fend for himself. He wanted to scoop her up and rain kisses on her worried face.

Fortunately, Poppa emerged from the gathering mist with two thralls. One was Bryk's personal slave, Torstein, the other a burly Irishman belonging to Poppa. Padraig took Hrolf's weight and staggered away with him. Bryk puzzled about the curious smile the Frankish concubine sent his way as she left. Perhaps it amused her he was burdened with three foreign women.

Cath-ryn came to him without hesitation and collapsed in his arms, teeth chattering. He put his arms around her, willing his heat into her body, relishing the feel of her against him.

"You're safe," she murmured, eyes bright with tears.

"*Ja*. Safe. *Hus*," he replied, cocking his head in the direction of the town.

Ekaterina tapped him on the shoulder. "Where is this house?"

He turned, coming close to laughing out loud at the sight of the elderly nun and Kaia huddled in his cloak. He brushed away a tear from Cath-ryn's cheek then let go of her, picked up Ekaterina and climbed out of the boat. "*Kom!*"

Both young women followed without hesitation, clinging together as they dogged his heels through the empty streets of the town.

Without being told, Torstein shouldered the heavy sea chest and fell in behind.

THE TRIPTYCH

The *house* Bryk had commandeered was a one-room hovel not far from the cathedral. Judging by the remnants of food and dirty wooden plates scattered here and there on the packed earth floor, Cathryn guessed the inhabitants had left in a hurry.

Bryk indicated to his servant where he wanted the chest. After putting it down with a thud in one corner, the young man quickly brushed aside the ashes inside a circle of stones in the centre of the dwelling. He wiped his hands on his tunic, then built a fire with kindling and wood piled nearby.

Bryk took what looked like the materials needed to strike a flame out of his pouch and threw them to his servant. "Fire," he said with a smile, rubbing Cathryn's upper arms. "Soon warm."

She wished she spoke enough of his language to tell him she needed only his touch to drive away the chill.

The cramped space filled with smoke as the servant blew on the spark, trying in vain to get a flame going. He looked at Bryk nervously. Kaia's hacking cough returned.

Cathryn hunkered down near the grate, ready to assist with the blowing. "Perhaps if I—"

Bryk grasped her arm and pulled her away. "Torstein do alone."

His gruff manner alarmed her. She thought to protest but caught Ekaterina's glance. "It's Torstein's responsibility," the elderly nun explained. "You mustn't interfere."

The expression on the youth's sooty face when the fire sprang to life reminded Cathryn keenly of the relief she'd often felt after satisfying *Mater* Bruna's demands.

Bryk unclenched his jaw and spat out a command to Torstein, who left the cottage quickly.

"Where is he going?" she asked.

Bryk lifted his fingers to his mouth. "Food."

Cathryn wondered how a young man who probably didn't speak the Frankish language hoped to find sustenance for them in a ransacked town. There would be food at the abbey, but she didn't want to be the one to lead the Vikings there. She shivered. They'd make their way up the hill in time.

There was no furniture, so they sat on the cold floor around the fire. She leaned on Bryk when he put his arm around her shoulders. As long as she was with him she was safe. She gazed across at Kaia. Her friend was too pale and still shivering despite the shaggy cloak in which she was cocooned.

It didn't seem long before Torstein returned. From the ensuing conversation she surmised he'd procured the large ham, the cheese wheel and the flagon of ale from Hrolf. Bryk seemed pleased by the news. The chieftain must hold him in high regard if he sent food. He took out his dagger and sliced off pieces of meat, handing them each a portion. Torstein broke the cheese wheel apart and laid it on the floor before retreating to the corner with the chest, though he didn't sit on it.

"Is he not hungry?" she asked, her mouth full of the delicious smoked ham.

Bryk frowned, but didn't turn to look at his servant. He lifted the horn he always carried off his body and poured ale into it. He took a swig before offering it to Cathryn. Her first taste of the bitter brew made her gasp. He motioned her to pass the horn to Ekaterina.

To her surprise, the old nun accepted it, drank a long draft, belched, then explained, "He will eat when we are done. It's the way of the Vikings."

She should have heeded the warning in the elderly woman's eyes, but instead she said, "Being a Viking's servant is obviously a hard life."

Ekaterina glanced at Bryk quickly then whispered. "Torstein isn't a servant. He's a slave."

~~~

Bryk was relieved to see color return to Kaia's ashen face after she'd eaten. Cathryn still leaned against him, but her body had stiffened at something the old nun had said. Everyone seemed to have eaten their fill. He'd have preferred some juicy roast pork and fresh white bread, but in the circumstances Torstein had done well.

He picked up three slices of ham and a chunk of cheese and threw them to his slave. He smiled as the youth grabbed them, stuffing everything into his mouth at once. Cathryn sat up straight, shrugging off his arm.

Frowning, he looked to Ekaterina.

"I told her Torstein is your slave," she explained.

Cathryn folded her arms, hugging her body.

"This upsets her?" he asked.

Ekaterina shrugged. "The Franks do not enslave their captives."

"Tell her Torstein was not a captive. He was born a thrall, as was his mother."

To his dismay, Cathryn still resisted his embrace when Ekaterina explained, but she said nothing and refused to look at him. It was a good thing he hadn't mentioned Torstein's mother had been sold off in the market at Ribe.

He touched his fingers to her chin and turned her face to him. He wanted her to understand the ways of Vikings, though why her opinion was important he still couldn't fathom. "Vikings, Franks, different ways. Not bad people."

Frustrated when her pout continued, he slipped back into his own language, depending on the old nun to explain. "Vikings spare the lives of captives. We feed and clothe, give them work, take care of their children. Franks do not show mercy to their prisoners."

She looked up at him with tear-filled eyes. "Better to be dead than a slave."

Her words cut his heart. "Should I have killed you then, that night?"

~~~

Exhaustion heightened Cathryn's confusion. Her wits had fled. Bryk's closeness caused joy to surge through her body, but fear held her in its grip. Did he intend to keep her as his slave?

She knew what obedience was, and humility, but she wanted more from this man who'd captured her heart as well as her body.

"No," she replied in a whisper. "I am glad to be alive, and here with you."

"*Da!*" Ekaterina exclaimed as Bryk smiled.

I will be his slave if it means I can be with him.

He squeezed her hand. "Look treasure now."

He motioned for Torstein to bring the chest. The thrall set it down at his side and opened the lid once Bryk had produced a key from his pouch and unlocked it. The corners of the young man's mouth twitched into a smile at first glimpse of the vestments on top of the pile.

Bryk slapped him on the shoulder, grinning broadly, then snaked his big hands under the garments and lifted them out.

She half dreaded he would get to his feet, unfurl the robes and put them on. Instead he set them aside and delved into the chest for something else. He handed a few candle ends to Torstein who pulled a glowing twig from the fire and lit them. Their soft flickering glow brought comfort to the dark hovel.

He then pulled out a misshapen chunk of candle still wedged onto a candlestick made of gold. He yanked it off to reveal a pointed holder as long as Cathryn's hand. He handed it to her. "For you."

Cathryn had never owned a personal possession. Nuns were forbidden attachment to worldly things. She longed to accept the gift, moved beyond imagining by the pleasure in his gaze. She wiped her palms on her skirts and glanced at Ekaterina. The old nun nodded.

With trembling hands she took the treasure from him. "Thank you."

It was heavy, an object of value. She should have been mortified that it had been plundered from a Christian church, but joy tingled up her spine as she slowly traced a finger from the base to the tip.

Kaia suddenly giggled. Ekaterina's face reddened. Bryk coughed, then held out his hand. "Keep safe. In sea chest."

She handed it back and watched as he nestled it into the folds of his extra clothing. Then he came to his knees and carefully unfolded the vestments.

The expectation on his face showed he thought there was something wrapped inside.

Ekaterina sucked in a breath when the object was revealed—an exquisite triptych, a small folding altarpiece. "Gilded copper," she breathed, "made for a rich patron."

Bryk traced a fingertip along the ornately curved top then carefully opened one of the wings to reveal the figure of a man embossed on the inside.

"Saint John Baptist holding a lamb," Ekaterina explained to Bryk. "The Baptist named his cousin, Jesus Our Lord, as the Lamb of God who would be sacrificed to redeem sinful humanity."

"Poppa has spoken of this lamb before," he said thoughtfully, stroking the animal.

Then he slowly opened the second wing. The center panel depicted Christ on the cross with Saint John and the Blessed Virgin Mary on either side.

Cathryn had expected this. What stole her breath away and had Ekaterina and Kaia exclaiming out loud was the scene engraved on the interior of the right wing—there was no mistaking the figure of Saint Catherine with her attributes of Sword and Wheel, symbols of her martyrdom.

Ekaterina launched into a mantra in some incomprehensible language, her eyes turned heavenward, hands raised in supplication.

Kaia burst into tears.

Cathryn stared at the triptych in disbelief. Her patron saint hadn't abandoned her.

Bryk sat back on his haunches, looking from one stunned woman to the next, obviously at a loss to understand what was happening.

Cathryn pointed to the panel, then pressed her palm to her breast. "Catherine is my saint."

The warmth of his hand over hers calmed her instantly. "Cath-ryn," he whispered, gazing at the artifact. "What is this?"

"Catherine was a princess who was scourged and imprisoned by the Roman emperor Maxentius because she refused to give up her Christian faith. Many people came to see her, including the Empress. All became Christians. Then, Maxentius proposed marriage."

Cathryn waited while Ekaterina explained these details, wondering if she had the courage to tell him the rest of the story. Bryk nodded thoughtfully, then looked to her.

She swallowed hard. "She refused, declaring she was the bride of Jesus Christ, to whom she had pledged her virginity."

Ekaterina hesitated, but somehow managed to convey the details to Bryk. Was he blushing?

She gathered her courage. "The furious emperor condemned Catherine to death on the spiked breaking wheel, but, at her touch, this instrument of torture was miraculously destroyed. Maxentius finally had her beheaded." She sliced her hand across her neck, smiling weakly.

Bryk remained silent for long minutes. Many of the candles guttered out. Only the glow of the embers lit his pensive face. Ekaterina fell asleep, snoring softly. Kaia dozed, slumped against the wall. Torstein gazed into nothingness.

Her Viking turned to look at her, his hand resting on the figure of the saint. "You are like her. Brave."

~~~

Bryk had stood at a fork in the road of life before. He'd made the decision to turn away from murder and mayhem. It hadn't been easy. Myldryd might still be alive if he'd chosen differently.

Whichever path he chose now might lead to destruction. The cult of the White Christ that he and his compatriots mocked perhaps had more to it.

What caused a god to sacrifice his son? Some of the Norse gods he revered seemed like a gang of squabbling *nithings* in comparison. Why had the saint held fast to her faith despite the threat of torture and death? She'd claimed to be the bride of Christ and remained faithful to her husband.

Myldryd had abandoned him, unable to face being shunned by her family. Would Cath-ryn be willing to give her life for him? Deep in his heart he believed she would sacrifice herself for someone she loved, but these musings were a waste of time. He could never marry a captive, a foundling at that.

If he abandoned the Viking gods, he would never feast with Odin in Valhalla, nor with Freyja in the banquet hall of Fólkvangr.

Cath-ryn had fallen asleep against him. He watched her breasts rise and fall, listening to her steady breathing. That she felt safe enough to sleep calmed his troubled heart.

He eased down to lie on his side, drawing her into his arms, then pulled the heavy Christian robes over them. She murmured something and cuddled into him.

Need pounded in his loins like Thor's hammer. Why not take her now? This woman fired his blood, stoking desires dormant since Myldryd's death.

But she was an innocent, and rape lay like a grim ghost deep in his bones, reminding him of the evil he'd once been capable of. Christians preached the forgiveness of their god, but was there salvation for a man haunted by past misdeeds?

She wouldn't fight him, he was certain. She was his, but their bodies would join for the first time on a bed of thick furs, in private, crying out their fulfillment. He liked the notion of watching Cath-ryn scream in ecstasy.

His already hard *pikk* turned to granite. He'd get no sleep this night.

SIMPLE THINGS

Cathryn stretched lazily, then startled. It was fully light. She and the other sleeping nuns remained in the hovel, but she was the only one covered by a mound of priestly robes. She threw them off, guilt and panic gripping her heart. Where was Bryk? Had he abandoned her?

A slight movement in the corner caught her eye. Torstein sat cross-legged, watching.

Bryk had left his thrall to guard her—and his chest was still where he'd left it, the padlock hanging open.

A memory of his gift—the first she'd ever received—drifted back. It had been too dark to see the candlestick and the triptych properly. An urge to touch them again seized her.

She crawled over to the chest on all fours and put a hand on it. Torstein scurried to her side. She assumed he would stop her, but he opened the lid.

"Thank you," she said. "*Takk.*"

He looked at her curiously, then retreated back into his corner.

She was lifting out the precious objects when Bryk entered the dwelling. He eyed her suspiciously.

"I wanted to see them again," she explained, feeling her face redden. Did he think she meant to steal his possessions?

To her relief he smiled, coming to kneel beside her. "You like?"

It was on the tip of her tongue to tell him she loved them, that she loved him, but God might strike her dead for coveting stolen religious objects, and for loving a pagan.

He was a warrior, a barbarian who would laugh at the idea of a silly girl pining for him.

Ekaterina and Kaia stirred from their slumber.

Bryk put the loot aside and removed two water skins slung across his body and gave one to Torstein, along with a small sack. The slave scurried off to rekindle the fire.

"For apples," Bryk explained with a smile, holding up the second water skin. He took all his possessions out of the chest to reveal a layer of sacking in the bottom. He removed the first layer. The three women stared at neat rows of twigs with their roots wrapped in straw. He touched the back of his hand to the straw, then sprinkled water from the skin over everything.

Then he carefully lifted the layer with the twigs. Below were hundreds of densely packed shiny black seeds. They glistened like the scales of a tiny dragon. Bryk picked up a handful, spread them in his palm and stared.

There was more to this man than she had ever imagined. "Why are apples important to you?"

Bryk touched a fingertip to the seeds in his palm. "In our legends, the goddess Ydun gives apples to the gods, thereby granting them eternal youthfulness. When I win land here I need something to grow people will want.

"In the legends of the Vanir, eleven golden apples were given to woo the beautiful Gerdr by Skírnir, who was acting as messenger for the god Freyr."

Cathryn was lost, despite Ekaterina's explanations. "Who are the Vanir?"

He blew into the air. "Njord is the god of the wind who fills our sails, important to seamen." He looked her in the eye. "His children Freyr and Freyja are the gods of fertility."

Ekaterina grinned naughtily as she explained the word that had rolled off his tongue like honey from the dipper.

"*Fruktbarhet*," Cathryn repeated, elated at his smile of pleasure.

"As well, the goddess Frigg sent King Rerir an apple after he prayed to Odin for a child. Frigg's messenger was a crow who dropped the apple in his lap. Rerir's wife ate the apple and bore a son—the heroic Völsung."

The only apple in the Christian tradition that Cathryn knew of was the fruit of the tree that symbolized Adam's fall from grace. Bryk's legends were richer, more in tune with the life giving and healthy properties of the fruit.

The stories were an important part of his history and culture. Their backgrounds and beliefs were very different, perhaps too different. What did he think of her God his people called the *Vite Krist*? "Too many strange sounding names," she murmured weakly.

He rummaged through his pile of belongings and drew out a small silver pendant. The circular keepsake with the figure of a woman at its center lay like a fragile jewel in his palm. He held it out to her. "For you," he said, pointing to the woman. "Freyja."

Cathryn accepted the precious object with trembling hands. It was a woman's talisman. Who had it belonged to? His mother or his wife? She feared any attempt to utter words of thanks would reveal her longing to know more about him.

"My wife's," he said, his eyes bright.

Cathryn smoothed a finger over the goddess, deafened by the frantic beating of her broken heart. "What is her name?"

"Myldryd," he rasped. "She died."

~~~

Shackles fell away as Bryk spoke his wife's name out loud for the first time since her death. He was seized with a desire to tell Cath-ryn the whole story, to reveal fears and torments he'd never shared with anyone.

But he hadn't learned enough of her language, and these were things he wanted to whisper without an elderly woman as a go-between.

However, he could share some of the things he'd brought from Norway. He found the ceramic oil lamp his mother had made when he was a boy, small enough to fit in his palm. "Light," he explained as they passed it from one to the other.

The tiny flute he'd fashioned from the bone of a goat needed no explanation. Cath-ryn's eyes filled with tears as the plaintive notes emerged from an instrument he'd sworn he would never play again after the child he'd made it for was lost. He wasn't sure why he'd brought it with him, but was suddenly glad he had.

Her tears turned to laughter when he switched to the jaw harp, a memento of a journey to Pomerania. He laughed with her, rendering it difficult to keep playing. When was the last time he'd laughed? Even the sullen Kaia seemed caught up in the merriment as she held Ekaterina's hands, steadying the old woman who danced tottering steps to the resonant twang of the instrument.

Winded, Ekaterina sat down heavily, a gleam in her eye when he located his *hnefatafl* board and playing pieces. "*Da!* I know how to play," she exclaimed, then rushed into an explanation of the rules partly in the Frankish tongue, the rest in some language only she understood.

But he caused the biggest uproar when he produced a glass mirror and a comb made of deer antler. For a moment he feared the three women might come to blows over who should get to use them first. He held up a hand to calm the squabbling and handed the mirror to Ekaterina.

~~~

There were no mirrors in the convent, and Cathryn suspected this was the first time in many a year Ekaterina had seen her own face. She stared into the glass, barely touching her fingertips to her forehead as she traced the deep wrinkles. Cathryn wondered if she would remove the coif and wimple she had steadfastly clung to, but it was a forlorn hope. Instead, the nun smiled broadly and exclaimed, "Still a beauty!"

Everyone laughed with her. "*Ja!*" Bryk said with a smile that made her throat go dry. He handed the comb to Kaia. Cathryn pouted at her smug friend, but was secretly glad he had left her to the last.

Kaia tugged the comb through her tangled hair, preening this way and that as she looked into the mirror then reluctantly handed the items over.

Cathryn noticed some sort of decorative lettering along the spine of the comb. She traced a finger over it. "This looks like Greek. What does it say?"

Ekaterina clucked. "Not Greek. Runes."

"It says *Bryk Gardbruker made this*," he rasped, covering her hand with his and guiding her fingertip over the symbols.

"You made it?" she asked, savoring the warmth of his skin and filled with reverence for the fine carving that must have taken hours of patient work. "And the mirror?"

He shook his head. "Trade."

Then he delved into the pile again, this time producing a tiny silver spoon no bigger than her little finger—too small to use even for a quail's egg.

When she looked at it curiously he put it to his ear and rotated it. "For cleaning," he explained.

If she still harbored the notion of Vikings as crude barbarians it disappeared like a puff of smoke. Her admiration for these resourceful people increased when Torstein brought forth steaming bowls of barley porridge he'd quietly boiled up on the fire.

CHOICES

In the late afternoon, Bryk mounted Fisk. Torstein lifted Ekaterina into his arms. She beamed up at him as he nestled her on his lap. He smiled back.

Cathryn and Kaia fell in behind as the horse, led by the slave, walked slowly up the hill to the abbey. Fifty Viking warriors followed.

Ekaterina had said nothing, but Cathryn recognized in her heart the old nun would want to live out her days at the convent. Communicating with the Vikings would henceforth be more difficult. However, Bryk was quickly learning her language and anxious to speak it at every opportunity. Somehow they seemed to understand each other.

And there was always Poppa and Hrolf.

The chieftain and his wife and son led the procession. She hoped Hrolf's presence wouldn't be too intimidating for the people who'd sought refuge in the abbey. He had agreed with Bryk on the importance of normal life resuming as soon as possible. "There can be no prosperity without people," Bryk had argued.

"And certainly no progress without the support of the Christian clerics," had been Hrolf's reply. "Our intention to stay and rule this town and its environs must be made clear to the Rouennais."

To Cathryn's surprise, once they neared the abbey, the Archbishop of Rouen emerged from within the walls. She had seen him only once, at *Mater* Silvia's interment. He was tall, and dark-haired. Accompanied by several men in fine clothing, he walked forward, head held high. She had to admire his courage in facing the enemy, but supposed he hoped to dissuade the Vikings from sacking the abbey. He would also have watched the goings on in the town from atop the hill, and known there had been no mass slaughter, no wholesale destruction.

Cathryn steadied Ekaterina as Bryk lowered her to the ground before dismounting.

"Very strong, your Viking," the elderly nun whispered, her face flushed.

She didn't have a chance to reply that Bryk wasn't *her* Viking. Hrolf's booming voice rang out. "I am Hrolf Ganger. I have taken Rouen, and intend to rule here."

The Franks tried unsuccessfully to hide their surprise at the Viking's command of their language. Or perhaps they were amazed to be still alive.

The Archbishop stepped forward, his black robes billowing in the stiff wind blowing off the river. "I am Franco, Archbishop of Rouen. We are subjects of Charles, King of West Francia."

Cathryn hazarded a glance at Bryk, wondering if he'd understood the Archbishop's antagonist reply. His tightly clenched jaw and rigid shoulders indicated his dismay.

Hrolf, however, ignored the prelate's remarks. "Under my rule, Rouen will prosper. Norsemen work hard. Your people have naught to fear if they obey. There is to be no looting, no rape, no murder. You can continue to worship your god. Punishment for those who defy my commands will be severe, whether they be Frank or Viking. Lead the way from this place and return to your homes and churches. This is my command."

The Franks stared at Hrolf, then murmured amongst themselves for several long minutes before the Archbishop again came forward. "Since you purport to come in peace, we will obey, until King Charles arrives with his army."

Hrolf chuckled as refugees emerged from the abbey and walked to the downhill path, led by the Archbishop. "Rouen is ours," he told Bryk. "We won't wait for Charles the Senseless. We'll take the fight to him."

As Ekaterina explained Hrolf's words, Cathryn studied the walls of the only place she had ever lived, suddenly catching sight of *Mater* Bruna in the doorway. There was no mistaking the wrath in the Superior's scowling gaze. It appeared that a former postulant clad in Viking garb was a greater irritation than the historic scene unfolding before her.

A sense of smug satisfaction welled up in Cathryn's heart as she smoothed a hand over her scarf. But a leaden ball of dread settled in her belly when it struck her Bryk might leave her here.

~~~

Soon, only Bryk, his three Frankish captives and a scowling nun lurking in the entryway of the convent remained atop the windswept hill. Torstein waited a little way off with Fisk.

Bryk pondered what to do with Cath-ryn. He could ask Hrolf to station him in Rouen as part of the occupying force, but that would lessen his standing in the chieftain's eyes, and diminish his chances of a generous land grant in the future.

Life on the march with a marauding army was no place for a woman.

The peasants whose hovel they'd commandeered would soon emerge from hiding and return to their dwelling.

But he craved Cath-ryn's company, and her body. She was already an essential part of his happiness. If he left her at the abbey, he might never see her again.

A tug on his sleeve interrupted his thoughts. He looked down at Ekaterina standing on tiptoe, lips pursed to kiss him. He smiled and bent for her to peck him on the cheek. "Goodbye, bold rover. Take good care of Cathryn."

Then she was gone, waddling off towards the convent. She embraced Cathryn briefly, then took Kaia's hand and disappeared through the doorway. Neither woman exchanged greetings with the crow-like sentinel at the gate.

Cathryn stood alone like a stone pillar buffeted by the wind. She had her back to him, but he sensed her indecision. This was where she had spent her life. His heart admitted reluctantly she had to make the choice. Would she yield to the insistent scowling gaze of the crone and return to the safety of the convent, or turn to him? He prayed to Cath-ryn's patron saint that she would give herself over to him.

What?

Praying to a Christian martyr? What about the *Forn sidr*, the ancient practices and beliefs of his people? Lust had robbed him of his wits. He had nothing to offer a woman, especially a Frank, a captive.

But one day you will.

Where had such a thought come from? Was Freyja urging him on, or had the martyred bride of the White Christ heard his plea?

Through the fabric of his shirt, he fingered the square amulet hanging around his neck. Myldryd's half of the talisman lay buried in a grave far away. He whispered the words etched in delicate runes on its copper surface. "Think of me, I think of you. Love me, I love you."

Cath-ryn turned slowly to face him. "Please don't leave me here," she said hoarsely. "Take me with you."

He should have refused, should have admonished her to return to the convent, to the life she knew. But the relief rushing through his veins as he gathered her up and signaled Torstein to bring Fisk overwhelmed his better judgment. No matter the difficulties, he would protect this woman.

All shall be well.

Fury twisted the crone's face as she glared in their direction then whirled to enter the convent. The door shut with a resounding bang behind her.

As they rode back down the hill, the sun came out and the wind calmed. To be safe, Bryk thanked first Freyja, then Odin, then Cath-ryn of Alexandria for the gift of this beautiful woman who had brought light to his dark life.

A NORSE WEDDING

Once the Rouennais and their Viking conquerors had reached the town, Hrolf commandeered part of the Archbishop's residence as living quarters for his family. The cleric seemed visibly chagrined, but put on a brave face. Perhaps he was sympathetic to Poppa's plight as a former Frankish noblewoman captured by Norsemen.

Bryk had urged Fisk to move on but reined to a halt when Poppa called to him. "There will be a chamber here for you and your captive. The Archbishop is aghast at the notion of your taking her into the town, and I agree. Have you explained *more danico* to her?"

He shook his head, relieved she had spoken in his tongue, though he suspected from Cath-ryn's red face she understood the gist of what they were saying.

"You must tell her," she insisted.

He dismounted quickly and put his hands on Cath-ryn's waist. He lifted her from the horse, savoring the touch of her hands gripping his shoulders and the softness of her warm body as she shyly pressed it to his. He doubted she was aware of what the hard flesh at his groin meant.

"Tell me what?" she asked, her hands moving to his biceps.

He gestured towards the dwelling. "You, me, we live here."

She narrowed her gaze. "In the Archbishop's house?"

"*Ja!*"

"You and me? Together?"

"*Ja!* Together."

"But we're not married." She looked to Poppa. "Explain that I cannot live in sin with him, especially here."

Poppa's reply wasn't what she expected.

"You won't be living in sin. Hrolf and I have never married, except in *more danico,* which is to say in the tradition of the Norse tribes. It's the only way a Viking nobleman can join with a foreign captive considered to be of lesser rank. Hrolf is the son of a *jarl,* I was the daughter of a Count—but a captive.

"It's their tradition, and if you want Bryk you must accept it. You have made your choice to give yourself to him. You are not of the nobility, yet he has chosen you. It's an honor."

The words whirled in the maelstrom of Cathryn's mind. "You and Hrolf aren't married?"

Poppa shrugged. "I suppose you can say I'm his concubine, since we have never had the blessing of the Church. But he has been faithful to me and I to him. He loves me, and I have come to love him. Someday, perhaps, when he embraces the one true faith—"

She glanced hurriedly at Bryk, and said nothing more.

"But your son—"

"Is Hrolf's heir. He never enslaved me."

She recalled Torstein had been born into slavery—a *fostri* Bryk had called him. Where were his parents? Were they both slaves?

She narrowed her eyes at her Viking, afraid he might believe she was rejecting him. "What does this mean? It's true I chose to be with Bryk, but I thought—"

He tightened his grip on her waist. "I want you," he rasped, his eyes bright.

What was it she saw in those brown depths? Love or lust? *Mater* Bruna had harangued the nuns often enough on the alarming subject of the inability of men to control their sinful urges.

But there was no room in her heart for guilt. "I want you, too," she murmured.

"Good!" he exclaimed. "Hrolf say the words, and you are mine."

~~~

Bryk had never thought to marry again. Myldryd had been given to him when they were children. His father had paid the bride price and signed the contract. They'd grown up knowing they would marry. They got along and he loved her, though he'd never burned for Myldryd the way he burned for Cath-ryn. When he was old enough, they'd undergone the ritual of bride buying and bride transfer, then celebrated with a feast. Essentially it was a commercial transaction between two families, and their marriage was much like everyone else's in Møre. They were comfortable.

It was accepted that if Bryk found a woman of higher rank he wanted to wed, he had the right to set Myldryd aside and remarry. But he'd known in his heart such a thing would never happen. For one thing, Myldryd was Hrolf's sister, the daughter of a *jarl*. For another, he was content with her.

She accommodated his needs, but he'd never thought of his wife as a passionate woman. She'd loved him in her own way.

He wanted to share these thoughts with Cath-ryn, but didn't have the words. He hoped his actions would show her he cared and would remain faithful.

If it were within his power he would participate in a Christian marriage, something she no doubt wanted with all her heart. But he'd have to forswear the Norse gods.

~~~

Cathryn had never given any thought to marriage, though she'd sung in the choir at two nuptial masses at the abbey. But her imaginings wouldn't have come close to the brief ceremony that had joined her to Bryk. She wished Ekaterina had been there to explain what was going on, but at least Poppa had helped her. The Frankish woman had supplied a fine linen chemise and woolen overdress, along with a traditional Norse headwrap.

She'd had no part to play. The men had done all the talking. Since she had no parents, Hrolf had given her away.

Representing his brother, Alfred gave Hrolf the vestments taken from the chapel of Saint-Éloi as her *bride price*.

The chieftain's eyes lit up as he shrugged his huge body into the too-small vestments and preened like a peacock. Poppa rolled her eyes.

Bryk presented her with the gilded copper triptych as his token of buying her. She should have been affronted by the notion, but the longing in his eyes when he handed it over touched her heart.

The feasting had already lasted much longer than the ceremony. The nervous Frankish servants had gradually relaxed as the evening wore on and the Norsemen hadn't slaughtered them.

She wondered if there was any food left in the kitchens after endless platters of venison, *jambon*, and vegetables had been served. How was it the Archbishop enjoyed such fare, certainly better than anything she'd ever eaten at the convent? The heat from Bryk's thigh pressed against hers shooed thoughts of hunger from her mind.

She'd never seen the heavily braided saffron shirt he wore, nor the tight leggings. When she'd commented on the absence of his usual leg wraps, he'd explained the leggings were kept in place by straps under the soles of his feet.

The notion of seeing something as intimate as the soles of his feet had her heart beating wildly, and the bulge at his groin cast into doubt unsettling things Poppa had told her about what took place in the marriage bed.

The silver pendant of the goddess Freyja hung around her neck. She rubbed the talisman between thumb and forefinger, finding it strangely calming.

At last, when she feared she might die of heat in the confined space of the dining area, Bryk held out his hand. "*Kom*, Cath-ryn," he said, his deep voice rich with promise.

~~~

For the first time in his life, Bryk wished he didn't belong to a tribe of men who were unashamedly vocal in their exuberance about sexual matters. He sensed his bride was skittish enough without the raucous cheers that echoed as he escorted his bride to their tiny chamber.

He had swallowed his pride and asked Poppa to arm him with words for the bridal bed, but hoped his lovemaking would demonstrate how much he cherished her.

Torstein had lit the candles as instructed, and the chamber smelled fresh, which was more than could be said when they'd first entered it earlier in the day. It had been a long while since he'd slept in a real bed and he trusted his thrall had made sure the linens were clean.

He didn't intend to do much sleeping this night. Cath-ryn had awakened a long buried desire to sire children, to perhaps establish his own dynasty.

He pulled off his boots, then casually eased the overtunic and shirt over his head and tossed them away carelessly. She'd seen him do this before, so he hoped she wouldn't be alarmed.

He knelt to remove her shoes. She watched, wide-eyed, her hands on his shoulders. Then she touched her fingertips to the silver amulets around his biceps. By rights they belonged to Alfred as the eldest son, but his brother had insisted Bryk have them.

"You were wearing these the night we met," she whispered.

"*Ja*," he replied. "My *fader*—warrior."

She stared up at the amulet around his neck as he came to his feet. "Can I touch it?"

His throat had gone strangely dry, so he simply nodded.

She examined the rune sheet. "It's green."

"Copper," he explained. "Green like your eyes."

"It has symbols, like the comb."

Was he ready to tell her he loved her, to explain Myldryd? "*Rún*," he replied, frustrated by his cowardice.

The silence stretched until she whispered, "You have nipples."

Her innocence struck him full force. The prospect of being the first to possess her was highly arousing, but he would have to be patient and careful not to hurt her. He sensed passion in Cath-ryn and Freyja had granted him the right to unleash it.

He took hold of her hands and put them on his chest. "Touch," he said. "Feel me."

He fervently hoped she would soon want to taste as well as touch him. She kept her hands where he had placed them for a few minutes, then brushed her thumbs over his nipples. He tilted his chin to the rafters, swallowing hard to smother the growl that threatened to emerge as desire spiraled from his sack into his spine.

She withdrew her hands quickly, her face full of concern. "Did I hurt you?"

How to explain the fire flowing through his veins at her touch? He decided to take a chance. He brushed his thumbs over the nipples pouting against the fabric of her dress. Her mouth fell open and she closed her eyes.

"Pain?" he asked.

She peeled open her eyes. "No," she replied hoarsely. "I like it."

She sucked in a breath when he did it again. Control of his greedy *pikk* was going to be difficult.

He put his palms over the brooches they'd used to pin the straps of her overdress, hoping he'd soon be cupping warm, firm breasts no man had ever touched. "Take clothing off."

She hesitated only a moment, then reached to unfasten the brooches.

~~~

To Cathryn's relief, Bryk took over the task of unpinning the elaborate silver fastenings from her trembling hands. The woolen overdress slipped soundlessly to the floor, revealing the fine linen chemise Poppa had given her. She'd never worn such a garment, but suddenly she wanted it off, wanted to feel the golden hairs on his chest against her skin. Were they soft or wiry?

Only a fool would think he'd never bedded a woman. She'd heard Vikings often had more than one wife. He would know what to do, because she surely didn't—yet she trusted him.

Her husband—should she call him that—raked his eyes from the top of her head to her toes. Her body heated under his gaze.

He motioned for her to raise her arms then reached for the hem of the chemise.

She did as he asked and he eased the garment over her head. The headwrap came with it. He buried his nose in the fabric, inhaling deeply before tossing it away. "Smell good," he said with a grin.

No one in the convent lingered overlong without clothing. Bodies were sinful earthly vessels to be kept covered. The nuns disrobed and dressed in the dark, and eyes didn't wander.

As a consequence, Cathryn had rarely seen her own body, yet now she stood calmly under the perusal of a lusty male. The hunger in his half hooded eyes produced tinglings in intimate parts she'd been taught to deny existed.

Bryk seemed particularly fascinated with her breasts. She had no inkling how they compared to other women's, but when he cupped her with his big hands, again brushing his thumbs over the nipples, the tingling turned to liquid fire.

She opened her mouth to ask if she was too small when he suddenly took her in his arms and crushed her to his body. The breath wooshed from her lungs as the heat from his chest flowed into her skin. His hair was soft. He didn't smell like the women she'd lived with. She supposed it was the scent of a man.

She clung to him as he carried her to the bed which was three times the size of her pallet at the convent, though she'd guess this was a seldom-used chamber for guests.

The linens were blessedly cool as he laid her down, but prickly heat flared again when he took her hand and pressed it to the swelling at the apex of his thighs.

If the rigid flesh she felt beneath her fingers was what Poppa had referred to as his *man part*, the woman had obviously fabricated the tale of it entering a woman's body.

He fumbled with the belt of his pants, his eyes darkening when the silver buckle refused to open.

He's nervous!

She climbed off the bed and reached for his waist. "Let me help."

He inhaled deeply, stretching his long neck as he'd done before, filling her with an inexplicable urge to lick it. She was afraid she'd offended him until he lifted his arms to the side. "Off, please, Cathryn," he growled.

~~~

Bryk was impatient with himself. He was too aroused, acting like a youth with his first girl. He'd come close to spilling his seed at first sight of the black curls at her mons. If he didn't get his leggings off soon—

Things were progressing too quickly. As she was unfastening his belt and he was sifting his fingers through her hair, the thought occurred that perhaps he should forewarn her. Try as he might the Frankish word for *big* eluded his frenzied brain. But then he became aware she had already hooked her thumbs in the waistband and was easing his leggings over his hips.

"Cath-ryn," he rasped, realizing when she gasped it was too late.

He quickly shucked the garment, giving thanks to Freyja he'd had the foresight to wear leggings and dispense with the leg wraps. She fixed her wide eyes on his erection. Then she took him completely by surprise when she cautiously touched a finger to the swollen tip of his rampant *pikk*. "It's very big."

By Odin. This woman will kill me!

Then she tried unsuccessfully to encircle him with her fingers. "And thick," she breathed.

He was lost. There were many things he wanted to tell her, but didn't have the Frankish words. He lapsed into Norse, hoping she'd understand. He braced his legs, then curled her hand around his manhood. "Your touch sets me on fire," he whispered near her ear. "Move your hand on me, like this."

Their bodies shared a language of their own. She responded and her skin heated as she learned his needs.

The faint aroma of female arousal wafted into his nostrils. He'd wager she was already wet. Intimacy with Myldryd had never been an earth moving experience. His raging desire for Cath-ryn put him in mind of a seething volcano he'd once seen in Iceland.

He'd planned to introduce her to the delights of tasting each other's intimate parts, but his need was too great. They had a lifetime to look forward to.

He scooped her up and laid her on the bed, opened her legs, pushed up her knees and knelt between them. She blushed as he stared at a part of her body she had probably never seen, her face as pink as the pretty wet folds. Perhaps he had time for one lick.

She dug her nails into his scalp, whimpering when he swiped his tongue over the glistening bud.

"I must have you now," he babbled half in Norse, half in her language, his voice raw. "Next time more slowly. I'll try not to hurt you but there will be pain."

She smiled like a Valkyrie come to take him to Odin's feast, which he hoped meant she'd understood. No time to worry about it.

He positioned his *pikk* at her fragile entrance, gathered her to his fevered body and plunged into her sweet, wet heat.

She screamed, clinging to him as he thrust and thrust and thrust. His mind filled with the memory of his heart hammering in his chest with awe and excitement as he'd watched the volcano hurl its molten lava skyward. Still he thrust, ever deeper, praying to Saint Catherine he wasn't hurting her too much. He gradually became aware she was keening out a long low wail that sounded like—

She threw her head back and stopped breathing altogether, trying to stammer something unintelligible.

She has released! Thanks be to all the gods and all the Christian saints.

It was his last coherent thought before his seed exploded inside his wife's pulsating sheath.

PART TWO

THE BEGINNING

Cattle die, kinsmen die, all men are mortal.
Words of praise will never perish, nor a noble name.
~The Havamal (Viking Book of Wisdom)

THE VIKING'S CONCUBINE

One month later

The apple tree sapling was dead, its grey leaves twisted grotesquely as if it had died in agony.

Fighting tears, Cathryn sank back on her heels in the brown dirt of the Archbishop's kitchen garden. Despite her best efforts to follow her husband's instructions for the care of his plants, it was the third one to shrivel within a sennight. At this rate, they'd all be gone by month's end. Rootstocks that had survived a perilous journey by sea from Norway to Francia seemed determined not to thrive in the rich soil of the Seine valley.

Witnessing Bryk's boyish pride in his newly planted apple trees had made her love him even more, if that were possible. Then he'd left with the Viking army a month ago. She dreaded having to tell him on his return that she had killed his dream.

If he ever returned—

With trembling hands, she grasped the twig and eased the root from the brown earth. It had withered like the other two.

"What are you doing?"

She swiveled her head, taken unawares by a familiar voice she hadn't heard since she'd turned her back on the abbey convent. "Kaia!" she exclaimed, dropping the dead sapling as she struggled to her feet.

The friends fell into each other's arms. "It's been too long," Cathryn said hoarsely. "Let me look at you." She narrowed her eyes, wiping away a tear when they broke apart. "You're not wearing your habit."

Kaia smoothed a hand over the fine wool of her skirts. "Papa decided my education was complete, and *Mater* Bruna became an even more unbearable tyrant after you left. Who would want to become a nun under such a Superior? Besides I plan to marry Javune."

Cathryn wondered what Kaia's wealthy father thought of the notion of his daughter marrying a monk, but she held her tongue. "So you are free of the convent?"

Kaia grinned. "At last. I was hurt you didn't come to visit me after you left."

Cathryn frowned. "But I did. I was refused entry."

Kaia grasped her arm. "What! Why?"

Would her noble friend understand? "I am not welcomed anywhere in Rouen, especially in places of religion."

Kaia squeezed her hands, her eyes full of sympathy. "Because you married a Viking?"

Cathryn stared at her dirty feet. "Because I am a Viking's concubine."

Kaia's mouth fell open. "Concubine? How can that be? You are living in the Archbishop of Rouen's residence."

"His Excellency has no choice. The Viking chieftain commandeered this house and allowed me and Bryk to occupy a small chamber. The Frankish servants shun me, though I am one of their own."

"But you and Bryk married."

"Yes, but it was a Norse wedding, without the blessing of the Church. Bryk is not of our faith."

Kaia narrowed her eyes, anger darkening her fair face. "I hate the Church and its rules. My true love is languishing in the abbey at Jumièges, no doubt pining for me, condemned by his father to a religious life he loathes."

Cathryn looked around nervously, relieved no servants were nearby to overhear her friend's blasphemous remarks. Perhaps a change of subject was called for. She smiled weakly. "It's good to hear and speak my own language again."

"Do you see no-one?"

"Mostly Vikings. The chieftain's wife, Poppa of Bayeux, enjoys talking with me in the Frankish tongue. She had scant opportunity during her years as a captive in Norway. Otherwise I think she would shun me too, like the other Vikings."

"Why do they shun you?"

"I'm a Frank. They are living in uncertainty waiting to hear if Hrolf has been successful in securing a grant of land from King Charles."

Kaia rolled her eyes. "The Senseless."

Cathryn nodded. "Until then they don't know if they will remain in this foreign land where they want to settle. I shouldn't give the impression they all ignore me. Alfred's wife, Hannelore, is always glad of my help with her ten children now her husband is away."

"Alfred?"

"Bryk's brother. His family lives in the Viking camp near the river. The little ones are teaching me their language. Bryk also allowed Torstein to stay with Hannelore."

"Does he come here?"

"Sometimes. He's helped with the trees, but he's a slave who only speaks when spoken to. It's hard to know what he's thinking. I can't imagine being a slave. It's one of the things I find hard to understand about the Vikings."

Kaia hesitated before replying. "I have seen Poppa in the town. She comports herself like a princess with her son. You'd think she was governor of Rouen rather than Tormod."

Cathryn chuckled. "I think when Hrolf chose Tormod to hold Rouen in his absence both men knew who would really be in charge. After all, she was the daughter of a Count."

"Have you heard anything of the war?"

Cathryn shrugged. "The last news Poppa received from Hrolf wasn't good. The Vikings had abandoned the plan to besiege Paris in favor of sailing down the river Eure to attack Chartres. What have you heard?"

"My father says the same." She glanced around. "I think he hopes they succeed. I overheard him saying that life in Rouen has improved under their rule. People feel more secure."

Cathryn's sprits lifted. Perhaps there was hope that one day Vikings and Franks would live in harmony in the valley of the Seine. It was her husband's fervent wish—along with the apple orchard he dreamed of nurturing. She bent to retrieve the dead sapling. "I have killed another tree," she lamented, heartsick with longing for Bryk.

CHARTRES

May 911 AD

Overseeing the setting up of the camp on an island in the river Eure, Bryk thought back to the day he and his fellow Vikings had left Norway, hoping to wrest new lands from the Franks where they could settle.

Alfred emerged from the midst of the hubbub, brushing dust from his *kyrtill*. "You must be pleased with your rise in stature," he said without rancor.

Bryk scratched his beard. Had his brother read his mind? It was true he'd been an outcast in Møre because of a decision two years ago to turn his back on warmongering and help his brothers work the family farm. Plundering and bringing home spoils was all very well, and he'd done it successfully for years. But bloodletting for sport sickened him.

His chieftain's fury at his decision had led to him being shunned, resulting in the death from grief of Bryk's wife, Myldryd, Hrolf's sister. She'd taken their unborn child to the grave.

Alfred chattered on, his voice filled with pride. "Thanks to your singlehanded capture of the town of Jumièges and its abbey, Hrolf has made you his second in command of more than one thousand warriors preparing to attack the town of Chartres. You left Norway as Bryk the Farmer, now everyone addresses you as Bryk the Warrior."

"It does please me," he admitted. "Trusted warriors will be granted the best tracts of land by Hrolf if we're successful in gaining and keeping territory. There can be no going back to Norway. And what I win will be for all of us." He winked at his brother. "Including you and your ten children."

Alfred smiled, but then his face darkened. "If only Gunnar—"

Bryk shrugged. It was pointless to regret the past, to wish that their younger brother hadn't been swept away in last autumn's storm tide that had taken hundreds of lives. Better to speak of something else. "Much as I appreciate the responsibility Hrolf has bestowed on me, I'd rather be in Rouen tending our fledgling apple trees."

Alfred smirked. "It's not the trees you miss, though we did go to great lengths to bring the rootstocks and seeds across the sea."

Again his brother had perceived the truth. It was his new Frankish wife he longed for. He worried how she fared, alone. They had spent only a sennight together after their Norse marriage. "I had to get my hands in the dirt. You understand that, but planting and fussing over my precious trees in the Archbishop's garden took much of my attention. I wish now I'd spent more time with Cathryn."

"I miss Hannelore too," Alfred said, "but at least I know she's in the Viking camp, with people who will look out for her. And I told you it would be better to plant your trees with mine, so my wife and Torstein could take care of them."

Alfred had again sensed his worry. "I suppose I wanted to leave something of myself with Cathryn. I understand why the Franks treat me with disdain and mistrust, but it rankles that my bride has earned their censure by wedding me. In their eyes she is my concubine."

His first wife had died of shame, and Alfred was aware of it. Myldryd's death had brought him to his knees. "If I lose Cathryn there'd be no purpose to life. Norway holds naught but bitter memories."

The notion of securing fertile land and starting afresh in a new land had promised a way out of his darkness. Now a desire to find a place where he might establish a dynasty of his own consumed him. He and Cathryn would help Hrolf build a new country in this land of the Franks.

She was in his blood. Each time their bodies joined the dizzying passion left him filled with a serenity he'd never known. Just thinking of her caused pleasant stirrings in his *pikk*.

Alfred brought him back to the present. "That's what she is in the mind's eye of your fellow Vikings, brother. They look upon her as a concubine, beneath you in status."

"It's ironic she's my *captive* because I rescued her from Sprig, the monk who tried to rape her."

"Hannelore has offered friendship," Alfred said.

It was probably true, but Bryk suspected his sister-by-marriage welcomed another pair of eyes and hands to look to the demands of ten children.

He hoped the steadfast Christian faith his wife espoused would strengthen her. Behind his eyes he conjured an image of her kneeling in prayer before the gilded copper triptych he'd looted from the chapel of Saint-Éloi—his wedding gift to her.

She was perturbed one of the Archbishop's servants might discover it in their chamber, but refused to surrender it.

"She must feel isolated," Alfred said.

Bryk nodded. "We Vikings are proud of our ancestors and often share tales of them around the hearth. You and I have strong memories of our father and grandfather. Cathryn has no one. Yet she believes if the saint is with her, all will be well."

He supposed it was much the same as his belief that if the goddess Freyja smiled on him, he'd be a happy, fertile man. But this was no time to be daydreaming of children. He might soon be feasting with other fallen warriors in Odin's Valhalla.

Still he wondered if his seed had taken hold during the sennight they'd made love with abandon. The intuition that his virgin bride harbored a passionate nature within her had proven to be right.

He recalled the laughter they'd shared when he'd discovered a birthmark on her lower back she didn't know she had. She'd refused to believe him until he'd used his mirror to show her. His teasing had led to a confession that the women in the convent always rose and retired in the dark and were forbidden to look upon their own bodies.

He'd nicknamed it his *jordbær* because of its strawberry shape, and because she was so juicy, a notion that had spread a blush across her full breasts. He'd enjoyed sucking and licking it like the sweet fruit. That had led inevitably to—

Hrolf's sudden arrival in the camp, barking orders, took him by surprise. Bryk was tall, but the chieftain towered over him. If he made a habit of daydreaming about Cathryn and her strawberry birthmark during the coming siege the Franks would make short work of him.

Hrolf's gaze traveled quickly around the rapidly blossoming camp. He gave Bryk a hearty slap on the back. "You were right as usual, brother. These islands downstream of Chartres are a better place to set up camp. The heights of the town overlook those upstream. More vulnerable."

Bryk had thought his observations were common sense, and was astounded at the familiarity with which his chieftain addressed him. While it was true they'd been brothers-by-marriage in Norway, there'd never been any love between them. "We can keep them guessing here," he replied quietly.

Hrolf raked his nails through his bushy beard. "First order of business is to isolate Chartres by devastating its environs. I plan to leave at dawn with a good sized raiding party. You'll remain here to hold this position and send out spies. Get the men started building siege engines. The town appears more fortified than I remember."

Bryk wasn't surprised. The last time Vikings had attacked Chartres they had destroyed it. He too had noticed that the fortified walls came down to the river. Taking the town would be a challenge.

SUMMONED BY THE ARCHBISHOP

Hands clasped behind her back, Cathryn waited nervously in the Archbishop's private library, gazing round in dismay at the shelves crammed with codices of bound vellum and parchment of all shapes and sizes piled haphazardly. There were unbound sheaves too, some stacks threatening to topple at any moment.

She'd at first worried about the reason for her summons since she was normally ignored, as if she didn't exist. The chaotic disorder amid which she stood offered an inkling as to the reason for her presence.

The black-robed prelate swooped in, followed by a hooded monk. A shiver of fear raced up her spine at the memory of Sprig's attack, until the monk lifted off his cowl and looked up. She gasped. "Brother Javune!"

The young man bowed, smiling weakly, his eyes exhorting her not to reveal what she knew of him.

The prelate ignored her outburst. "I requested Brother Javune be allowed to travel from Jumièges to assist in setting the library to rights," he announced in a haughty tone, gesturing towards the shelves with bony fingers. "As you see, my predecessor left it in a less than desirable state."

Since Franco had been in office for nigh on half a year, she thought it inappropriate to lay all the blame for this mistreatment of precious books on Archbishop Witton, but said nothing.

He looked down his nose at her. "However, this young monk assures me you are the best person to examine the illuminated pages and restore those that are found to have deteriorated."

A tiny bud of hope sprouted in Cathryn's heart. She was to be allowed to work on sacred texts, doing something she loved and excelled at. Perhaps her fellow Franks hadn't written her off altogether. "I am humbled, my Lord Archbishop," she said hoarsely, finding the courage to look up at him. "It will be an honor."

He waved a dismissive hand, eyeing her Viking garb with distaste. "Yes, well, Our Lord welcomed Mary of Magdala so we mustn't condemn you too harshly. Those who repent their sins are to be forgiven."

She glanced up sharply at Javune. Beads of sweat had broken out on his forehead. He avoided her gaze. She suspected the Archbishop knew nothing of the young man's sin, of his apparent longing for Kaia.

Irritation welled up in her heart. The love she and Bryk shared wasn't sinful. Why did she need forgiveness? Was it wrong to love an honorable man because he espoused a different faith? Bryk's belief in his own gods was steadfast. He had pledged to her in the name of those gods, but because no Catholic cleric had blessed their marriage—

She shuddered, aware that voicing such heretical thoughts could lead to prosecution and perhaps death.

The Vikings suddenly seemed a tolerant people compared to her Catholic countrymen. Hrolf had allowed the Rouennais to continue practicing their religion. Bryk had never insinuated she should abandon her faith. In fact he seemed drawn to some aspects of it.

Still, she would seize this opportunity and pray that one day Vikings and Franks might live together in peace.

PREPARING THE SIEGE

It had been an exhausting few days for the Viking warriors, laboring under cloudless skies to build a siege engine.

Bryk and the men under his command had scoured the neighboring islands and the nearby banks of the Eure for suitable trees.

Cathryn had occupied his thoughts. Her strong faith intrigued him. She'd talked about forgiveness, about the son of her god dying for the sins of others. Bryk had a multitude of past sins preying on his mind. He regretted the marauding barbarian he had once been. Would Cathryn's god forgive him? He was certainly repentant.

Alfred's voice brought him back to the present. "I thought the long days of rowing had strengthened every muscle in my body," his brother complained, rubbing his biceps. "But I was wrong."

Bryk stretched his arms to ease the ache in his shoulders from wielding an axe for hours on end. "I know what you mean."

The air rang with the sounds of hammering as men pounded rivets pulled from one of the less seaworthy longboats.

"I'm certain this racket has alerted the people of Chartres to our presence and our purpose," Alfred said.

Bryk shrugged. "It can't be helped. Hopefully they won't be expecting a *sambuca* to arrive, bringing men from the water over the walls."

Stripped to the waist, they sat on the grass, sharing a waterskin, watching the completion of the platform that joined two of the boats together. It would form the base for the four foot wide *sambuca* that lay ready on the bank next to the boats.

Bryk stretched out on his back, squinting at the sun. The breeze felt good on his bare skin. It was the perfect day to be lying in the grass with Cathryn in his arms, or jumping into the river to cleanse his body of the sheen of sweat that coated his skin.

"I still think you should attach some sort of cover over the ladder," Alfred said. "Otherwise the Franks will pick the men off with arrows as they ascend."

Bryk dragged his thoughts back to the dreadful reality they faced. "No time. We'll have to carry shields with us," he replied reluctantly, aware his brother had no shield and no armor. "Don't worry. I'll make sure you're not in the vanguard."

A shout from downstream drew their attention. Alfred came to his feet, shaded his eyes and scanned the river. "It's Hrolf returning from raiding."

Bryk rose. "Let's hope he's had success and that he's pleased with our progress."

As they watched their chieftain's longboat approach, Bryk noted the look on Hrolf's face. It was one he knew well. It spoke of a bloodlust satisfied. The surrounding countryside had been laid waste. The siege was about to begin.

SPRIG

Cathryn was confident in her skill, but the Archbishop's intense scrutiny of her work was unnerving. He insisted on watching over her shoulder while she tried to repair a faded illumination.

He had fallen into the habit of visiting the library every day and seemed fascinated by the process, asking what seemed like a thousand questions.

It was bothersome that the queries weren't always about illuminating. She'd been shunned by her fellow Franks, yet was suddenly of immense interest to his Grace. She preferred the anonymity.

"*Mater* Bruna tells me you were a foundling at the abbey convent."

Perspiration trickled down the back of her neck, but she continued the careful quill stroke. "*Oui*, your Grace. I was left on the threshold in a basket."

"Hmm."

Hands behind his back, he strolled over to inspect what Javune was doing at the other *escritoire*. The rapid beating of her heart slowed, but then he glanced up at her sharply. "What year was that?"

She didn't dare look at his face. "I have almost nine and ten years, your Grace."

"And no one has any idea whose child you were?"

It was something she'd never considered until she'd met Bryk, a man full of proud tales of his ancestors.

"*Non*, your Grace," she replied wistfully.

"I see," he intoned gravely. "I see."

He paced back and forth for a few minutes, then left abruptly.

"Strange bird, that one," Javune observed. "I don't trust him."

Cathryn was inclined to agree, but it flew in the face of everything she'd ever been taught to decry a cleric. "He's an Archbishop. A servant of God."

Javune snorted. "You have noticed how well this servant of God lives, and yet I doubt if he has offered you payment for your work. He'd be hard pressed to find a better illuminator."

She warmed at the praise, but it dawned on her she'd never given any thought to such an idea.

"They can be the most untrustworthy, these men of God. Look at Sprig."

The mention of her attacker's name sparked fear in her heart. "But he is safely confined at Jumièges."

He shrugged, a look of pity in his eyes. "No, he isn't. He persuaded the Abbot you enticed him. Don't forget they are both from Neustria. Sprig was the Abbot's protégé at Vézelay Abbey. That's how he came to be at Jumièges."

Indignation soared up her throat. "You saw us together. I never did anything to encourage his attentions."

"I know, but Sprig played the part of the penitent sinner very well, and you are a mere woman after all, a daughter of Eve."

She spluttered, her mind a maelstrom of confused thoughts concerning Sprig. "Neustrian. No wonder he speaks the Frankish tongue with inflexion."

Javune nodded. "The Abbot is sending him back to Vézelay. He accompanied me to Rouen."

An icy fear crept up her spine. "What? He's here? Where is Vézelay?"

"About six days south, but he had to travel through Rouen and then follow the Eure."

"Isn't that the river that flows through Chartres?" she said hoarsely.

Javune seemed not to have heard her. "Besides," he continued, "the Abbot didn't consult me. My father has led him to believe I'm a ne'er do well. He thinks as the youngest son I should be happy to spend my life in God's service."

She took a deep breath, determined not to look away. "But you would rather be with Kaia."

The wretched desperation in his blue eyes reassured her that his feelings for Kaia were true. "I'm sorry," she said. "I know what it is to be separated from someone you love."

Javune scowled. "But at least you have gained your freedom. I am entombed and will never be free. You can walk away from here. I cannot."

She had once felt the same, but it struck her full force how fortunate she'd been to find Bryk. Her rescuer was a strong, determined man who would protect her with his life. If Javune left the monastery he would be a penniless outcast, fated never to marry Kaia.

The thought of Sprig being free and spreading lies about her right here in Rouen filled her heart with dread. She felt Bryk's absence keenly.

"If Sprig is a threat I should mayhap seek refuge in the Viking camp by the river," she murmured, knowing she wouldn't be welcomed with open arms. But they would protect Bryk's property.

A strange light lit his eyes. "Perhaps I should accompany you," he replied.

SIEGE ENGINES

The Vikings had spent an extra day building a railing on either side of the ladder, then heaved it into position so its foot rested across the sides of the two vessels lashed together.

It had taken fifty men to hold it with the other end protruding beyond the prows while the foot was hammered into place.

Beyond exhaustion, Bryk had slept the sleep of the dead, despite the battle that loomed. Everything was in readiness. In the pre-dawn darkness Hrolf gave the signal.

Rowers took up the oars on the outer sides and pulled the two vessels upriver to the walls of the town. They'd been picked for their strength; once the boats turned to face Chartres they had to keep them steady across the swift current.

Standing at the base of the ladder, legs braced, ready to lead the charge, Bryk held his breath. Many things could go wrong. He glanced up at the pulleys at the top of the masts, feeling the weight of his helmet. He hoped the ropes they'd made from the inner bark of trees would hold. They'd strengthened them with elk hide rope from their ships. He'd had to guess at the length of the ladder since he hadn't had the opportunity to properly view the fortified walls.

The prows of the longboats came close to the walls. "Up!" he yelled to the ten men standing on the sterns who then heaved on the ropes attached to the head of the ladder. Hand over hand they strained to raise the apparatus with the aid of the pulleys. Others on the prows assisted with the lifting of the machine, keeping it steady with long poles while the boats tossed beneath their feet.

Bryk slung his shield on his back and began the long climb as the ladder was being hoisted. Three men followed. The plan was to overpower the first defenders and secure the ladder once they reached the platform at the end.

The men behind him grunted with exertion as the climb became steeper. A hue and cry broke out above them when the enemy perceived the Vikings' tactic.

He looked down at the muddy shoals of the river Eure, and wished he hadn't. He inhaled deeply to settle his roiling belly. He'd never liked heights. Even harvesting apples made him dizzy.

The ladder lurched as the main body of attackers began the climb. He was confident the wooden structure would hold the weight, but the ropes were another matter.

He fixed his eyes on the top of the wall. It still seemed a long way away. His heart sank. He'd made the ladder too short.

~~~

Hrolf pouted for two days, pacing back and forth outside his tent while they labored to extend the ladder. He snarled at anyone who dared speak to him. Bryk decided it was better not to bother.

No mention was made of the sneering laughter of the town's defenders that had followed them as they withdrew the *Sambuca*.

Finally the chieftain came down to the water's edge. "We've put all our hopes on one siege engine. That was our mistake. The men can finish this job. I want you to build me a catapult, and a battering ram. We must leave nothing to chance."

It came as a relief that Hrolf apparently didn't blame him for the shortcomings of the *sambuca*, but a catapult would have to be built in full view of the town, and Bryk had never seen a battering ram, let alone crafted one.

Hrolf raised his hand. "I know. I'm asking a great deal. But if any man can accomplish this, it's you. Now let's get started."

CATHRYN SAILS WITH VIKINGS

The Viking sentries at the camp on the banks of the Seine recognized Cathryn and didn't challenge her, but were adamant Javune couldn't pass through the compound fence they'd constructed.

"He's a friend," she said gently, indicating his robes. "A man of God."

One of the sentries spat into the dust. "*Vite Krist!*" he exclaimed, impatiently beckoning Javune to move inside with her.

The encampment, normally filled at this time in the afternoon with the noise of children playing, bustled instead with activity, people rushing here and there.

"Something's going on," she told the young monk. "We must hurry to find Hannelore."

She'd feared Javune's habit would draw hostile glares, but no one paid attention to them as they pushed their way through the busy throng. Everyone seemed to be heading towards the river, laden with bundles and chests. "I have a terrible feeling they are leaving," she confided to her companion.

Javune looked afraid. "Mayhap they've lost the battle for Chartres and are fleeing back to Norway?"

Her heart hammered in her chest. The camp consisted of mostly women, children and thralls. "They would never make it back to their home country alive, and why would they want to without their men?"

The import of her words struck her full force. If Chartres had been lost—

By the time they reached Hannelore's tent, Cathryn was breathless and frantic. Her sister-by-marriage took her hands, looking worried. "What is wrong, Cathryn?"

It cheered Cathryn's heart that Hannelore had spoken, albeit haltingly, in her language, but she couldn't hide her consternation. "Are the Vikings leaving?" she asked.

Hannelore frowned. "Some leave. Go Chartres."

"Chartres?" she cried. "Why? What has happened?"

"Talk Poppa," Hannelore replied.

Cathryn looked to where Hannelore pointed. Chin tilted to the sky, hands fisted on hips, Poppa stood beside a longboat, surveying the activity around her as if she was Commander-in-chief of a mighty army. More astonishing was that she was clad in men's attire. Since Hrolf's clothing would have swamped her, and the leggings and tunic seemed to fit perfectly, Cathryn had a momentary notion the outfit belonged to Poppa.

"What is the arrogant woman doing?" she muttered to herself, already on her way down the riverbank.

Poppa waved when she saw her. "Cathryn!" she called huskily.

Was it her imagination or had the Frankish woman's voice deepened? Although relations between her and Hrolf's concubine had warmed over the past sennights, she was surprised by Poppa's apparent happiness at seeing her. "You're going to Chartres?" she asked.

The smile left Poppa's face. "The news from Hrolf is not good. They need more men."

Cathryn was afraid to ask about Bryk. She had to trust Poppa would tell her if he had perished. "But the warriors Hrolf left behind secure the town. We are mainly women in the camp," she pointed out.

"And hundreds of thralls. They are men. They can fight. I myself will lead them down the Eure."

Cathryn thought of Torstein. "What if they don't wish to risk their lives for their masters?"

Poppa looked at her in disbelief. "Then they will die in this foreign place. We are their protection."

Cathryn scanned the longboats, noting for the first time that thralls were indeed stowing their meager belongings, claiming their places. A desperate notion seized her. "Take me with you," she begged.

It was lunacy. She'd be sailing down an unknown river with hundreds of thralls heading for a town where military confrontation loomed large. But it would bring her closer to Bryk, and take her further from Sprig.

Poppa frowned at her in disbelief, but then softened her gaze. She eyed Cathryn from head to toe. "You will need different clothing. Go to my quarters. Padraig will see to it. Tell him I sent you. If the monk comes he'll be expected to row."

Cathryn had forgotten Juvane. She swiveled her head to see him standing uncertainly on the bank, his sandaled feet mired in the trampled mud. Surely he wouldn't want—

He nodded.

She turned back to Poppa who smiled. "Tell Padraig he'll need clothing also. The thralls will deem it an ill omen if he boards wearing that outfit."

Grinning broadly, Cathryn turned to run back to the camp, but Poppa caught her arm. "What of Bryk's apple trees?"

Panic lasted only until she saw the glint of amusement in the concubine's eyes. "I'm killing them anyway," she said, jubilant her husband still lived.

DISASTER

In the three sennights that Bryk and his crew labored to make the two siege engines, Hrolf attempted to seize the town with the *sambuca* three times.

The first time the top of the ladder reached the wall, the inhabitants cut down the four men on the platform after a brief skirmish and threw them off. If they weren't dead when they hit the water, they were by the time they were fished out of the river downstream.

The decision was made to fashion wicker shields woven from willow saplings to three sides of the platform. These would protect the four in the vanguard until they could be unfastened and thrown open to allow the attackers to secure the rampart. Bryk deemed it an ill-advised plan, but was told in no uncertain terms by an impatient Hrolf to keep his mind on the new weapons.

When the ladder reached the wall the defenders were ready with bundles of blazing twigs, which is exactly what Bryk had foreseen. They set the wicker shields on fire and four screaming human torches fell to their deaths.

Following this catastrophe, arrows rained down on the rest of the raiders on the ladder who were then forced to retreat.

These failures added to Hrolf's fury and increased the demand on Bryk to complete the other siege engines.

Apparently emboldened by the successful use of fire, the defenders poured pitch on the platform the third time the ladder reached the wall, then set fire to it, resulting in the destruction of well over half the apparatus and the deaths of twenty-five men.

That same night, Hrolf's worried captains gathered around a brazier. The summer heat was sweltering, but the glowing embers warmed Bryk's chilled heart.

The mood was somber. It was a long while before Hrolf made the speech they'd expected. "The *sambuca* isn't going to work. I know the Romans are reputed to have used it with success, but Chartres evidently isn't Syracuse."

Bryk leaned forward, forearms resting on his knees. He knew what was coming so decided to take the offensive. "The battering ram is ready, but the catapult will take a few days longer."

Hrolf stroked his beard. "We cannot afford to have this siege go on much longer. It's possible the Bishop of Chartres has already succeeded in getting emissaries through our lines. A relief force may already be on the way. I want to be inside those cursed walls when they arrive."

TORSTEIN

The longboats bobbed in the shady shallows, the tired crews enjoying a respite from the midday heat. Javune accepted the heel of bread from Torstein, broke it in two and offered half to Cathryn. She nodded her thanks to the thrall, aware they would have gone hungry without the slave's resourcefulness. The corners of his mouth edged up into a hint of a rare smile. He evidently considered himself her property in the absence of his master.

He'd secured a place in the boat for Javune and taken the young Frank under his wing, showing him how to row with the least wear and tear on his hands.

He'd miraculously produced a small chest for Cathryn to sit on amidships. She wondered what was inside and if he'd stolen it. She'd only ever seen him with a small haversack on his back that presumably held all his possessions.

"What would your Superior say if she could see you now?" Javune teased. "All dressed up in men's clothing."

Cathryn laughed, covering her mouth with her hand lest she project bread into the conversation. "And armed," she said, patting the dagger at her waist that Poppa had given her. "She'd be scandalized, as your Abbot would be if he knew you were plying the oars of a longboat down the River Eure."

Javune sobered. "He'll know soon enough."

Cathryn watched Torstein out of the corner of her eye, suspecting he understood more of their conversation than they assumed. "You can never return, you know."

The runaway monk gazed around at the sluggish river then popped another piece of bread into his mouth. "Of that I am glad. If I die during this adventure, at least I'll have tasted a little bit of freedom."

Torstein snorted, then turned away.

~~~

She and Poppa were surrounded by hundreds of men, but Cathryn didn't feel threatened. She was confident that none of the thralls would dare lay a finger on Poppa. If they managed to overpower Padraig they'd still have to face Hrolf's wrath when he found out. In addition she knew Torstein lurked nearby, always vigilant. It was strange that he seemed to have adopted her.

"Can I ask a question about Torstein?" she said to Poppa as they bedded down for the night under a canvas shelter. Men's voices drifted on the still air. Nightjars called to each other in the distance. Crickets chirped. Frogs croaked.

"What do you wish to know?"

"His parents. Are they dead?"

Poppa shrugged. "His mother was sold off in the market at Ribe on the journey here."

Cathryn's heart broke for the youth. "I was a foundling, but to be torn apart from one's mother, never to see her again must be worse. Did they get the chance to say goodbye?"

Poppa stared at her as if she'd spoken in Greek. "He's a slave. Why do you care?"

Cathryn's first reaction was to think that twenty years with Vikings had changed Poppa, but then it dawned on her the haughty Bayeux countess had probably never cared much about the feelings of ordinary people. "What about his father?" she asked, regretting she'd embarked on the conversation.

"Swept away in a storm surge last autumn," she said with a yawn. "His name was Gunnar Gardbruker."

A chill crept slowly up Cathryn's spine, despite the fetid summer air. Surely it must be a common name. "Was he related to Bryk?"

"His brother," she replied sleepily.

CAPTURED

Poppa called a halt just before a bend in the river. At her command the thralls steered the boats to the bank.

Cathryn jumped over the side of her longboat into the shallows, enjoying the freedom male attire provided, and hurried along the bank to where Poppa stood at the prow. Torstein shadowed her. "Why have we stopped?" she asked breathlessly.

"Listen."

She strained to hear what Poppa had evidently heard. "Nothing. Only birds."

"Exactly. It's too quiet. We must be nearing Chartres, yet there is no sound, just a cloud of dust to the southwest."

Cathryn peered into the distance. "Mayhap it's smoke from Viking campfires, or from cooking fires in the town."

Poppa shook her head. "It's dust. Vikings don't make dust. Horses do. We must be careful not to sail headlong into any relief force that may be on its way to Chartres."

Cathryn looked around nervously. Who knew what lurked in the tall reeds? "A relief army? Who would march to relieve Chartres?"

"I suspect not King Charles," Poppa sneered. "But Hrolf feared Richard, Duke of Burgundy and perhaps Robert, Margrave of Neustria might respond to any plea for help from Bishop Joseaume of Chartres. Our hope is that only one may have decided to join the fray and that they haven't united their forces."

Cathryn's heart plummeted. Bryk faced enormous dangers. She'd known that, but in Rouen it had all seemed unreal. Now that she was so close to him, her fear intensified.

Poppa raised a foot to the rail of her boat. Padraig heaved himself over the side to assist her onto shore. As he set her back on dry land, he grunted and slumped to the ground. Cathryn screamed when she saw the arrow embedded in his back, but Torstein's surprisingly strong arm encircled her, pulling her away.

Helmeted men in chain mail emerged from the trees. Frankish soldiers! "Let her go," one of them shouted.

She stumbled backwards into Torstein, unable to keep up with his frantic pace. They fell in a heap. The boy struggled to escape from beneath her, but didn't utter a word. She opened her eyes to see the point of a sword poised above her head.

"Thank God," Poppa screamed in the Frankish tongue. "These barbarians captured us."

The soldier who'd been intent on killing Torstein took his eye off the thrall for a split second, but it was time enough for the slave to slip away into the forest. The soldier put away his weapon and raked his eyes over her, then took her hand. He pulled her up so forcefully she had no choice but to fall into his arms. He misunderstood her sob. "You're safe now. We're Franks."

Poppa was holding forth, arms flailing, shrieking about being noblewomen from Rouen captured by Vikings.

Many thralls had fled into the forest. Some of the soldiers had gone off in pursuit, but others armed with swords and spears herded the remaining thralls out of the boats. She couldn't catch sight of Javune among them. She prayed fervently their lives would be spared and that Torstein would evade capture. The Frankish soldiers seemed to have no idea they'd stumbled upon a horde of slaves. Perhaps to them one barbarian was much like another.

~~~

Cathryn and Poppa were forced to walk the dusty mile or so to the Frankish camp with the more than a hundred other captives, but weren't bound. Poppa continued to demand respect, protesting loudly that she was a highborn member of the Frankish nobility. Since it was the truth and she spoke the language, she carried it off well, but it was evident the soldiers were suspicious.

The size of the enemy camp astounded Cathryn. There were hundreds of tents and pavilions with soldiers milling around everywhere. The air was filled with fine grit that coated her dry lips and burned her eyes.

They were allowed a few sips of water from a skin, then ushered into a small canvas shelter and left alone.

Poppa peeked out. "The Franks are corralling the thralls into a roped off area out in the full sun. They're packed together like ling cod teeming in the net."

Cathryn wiped her cracked lips with the back of her hand, still thirsty despite the water. Fear lodged like an apple in her throat. "What should we do?"

Poppa paced. "Those recently enslaved may betray us. The ones born into slavery will not. We must continue to play the part of innocent captives if we want to escape and aid our men."

Cathryn thought of Torstein. Would he return to help them if he still lived? Or would he take advantage of a chance for freedom and disappear into the valley of the Seine? He was resourceful enough to possibly survive and begin a new life.

The camp remained unnervingly quiet for what seemed like hours. Cathryn dozed fitfully, sweltering in the stuffy tent. Poppa kept watch through the edge of the door flap. Suddenly she hissed at Cathryn. "The Franks are beginning their interrogation of the thralls."

Rubbing grit from her eyes, she scurried over to Poppa's side and peered out. In a dusty, grassless clearing about fifteen yards away two men in armor sat on elaborately carved wooden chairs that seemed ridiculously out of place in the middle of nowhere. It was evident from their bearing these were noblemen. "Who are they?" she asked.

Poppa inhaled deeply. "My guess is Richard of Burgundy and Robert of Neustria."

It was like a punch in the belly. "They've joined forces?"

Poppa offered no reply, and Cathryn sensed she too struggled with this new development. Poppa of Bayeux had the advantage of noble birth. Cathryn was a foundling who doubted she'd even be able to utter a coherent thought when questioned.

"They are bringing out the first of the thralls," Poppa said. "Your monk is among them."

Cathryn looked back once more at the horrific scene unfolding. Javune had been stripped to the waist, his hands bound. A soldier was dragging him like a dog on a leash towards the seated noblemen. Her heart stopped beating. She couldn't take her eyes off his bared back. At the base of his spine was a large birthmark that looked alarmingly like the *strawberry* on her own *derrière* that Bryk loved so much.

~~~

"Let's begin with the lad who purports to be one of us," the taller nobleman said, so softly Cathryn had to strain to hear, her thoughts full of her recent discovery. The mark on Javune's back meant nothing. Many people had birthmarks they kept hidden. Some considered them the mark of the devil.

Javune was dragged forward and made to kneel. Cathryn's thoughts went to Kaia. Impossible as their love seemed, she prayed the young monk might be spared punishment for her friend's sake.

"What is your name?"

Javune didn't raise his head. "I am Brother Javune Crochette, from the Abbey at Jumièges."

The nobleman leaned forward to grasp Javune's chin, tilting his face to his view. "If you are who you say, you should know enough to address your betters in the proper manner. I am Robert of Burgundy."

"*Oui, milord*," Javune rasped.

The Duke studied his face. "How do you come to be in a Viking longboat on the River Eure?" he asked.

"I was forced. My abbot sent me to Rouen to assist the Archbishop with his library. The Vikings control the town. They pressed unwilling citizens into service."

Burgundy scanned the imprisoned Vikings. "Yet you are the only Frank among them."

Cathryn held her breath. "Why didn't he say he was taken with us?" she hissed between gritted teeth.

"The mind doesn't always work quickly when one is afraid," Poppa replied with a shrug.

The other nobleman, presumably Robert of Neustria, leaned closer to Burgundy, but it was impossible to hear what he said.

"What of the women who claim to be nuns from Rouen?" Burgundy asked.

"They are from the Abbey Convent of Saint Catherine," Javune replied.

Neustria raised an eyebrow as he came to his feet. He drew his sword and touched it to Javune's throat. "One woman as pale as driven snow, and the other who looks to have lived life in the open air? And how do they come to be dressed as men?"

Cathryn had to turn away, too terrified to watch the interrogation. She feared Javune would falter, or die trying to protect her and Poppa. She dreaded to think how she would fare when they turned their attentions to them.

"They are from Rouen," Javune repeated.

"He's lying."

Cathryn's belly clenched. She had heard the voice before, and knew instantly who had spoken.

Sprig!

She looked back to the clearing. A monk in black robes stood next to Burgundy's chair. He was hooded, but she knew him all the same.

"Both women are concubines of Viking invaders. Javune here used to be a monk, but he has forsaken his calling and thrown in his lot with barbarians. They are traitors to their religion."

Poppa gasped, her face a mask of fury. "In all my years with Hrolf, I've held fast to my religion."

Her words jolted Cathryn. An image of her patron saint, defiant in the face of the spiked breaking wheel appeared behind her eyes. Her fear drained away as she came to her feet and took Poppa's hand. "Come, my lady. Let us face the fate that awaits us, but with the truth as our ally."

RECONNAISSANCE

The mood in the Viking camp on the Eure was somber. The gates of Chartres had easily withstood the first assault with the battering ram.

It had taken three exhausting days to find, fell and bring back to camp the huge log. Bryk's design called for a canopy to be built over the ram. Covered with wet hides from the cows they'd slaughtered and eaten, a canopy would have protected the men carrying the ram and prevented it catching fire.

The walls of Chartres rose steeply almost directly from the riverbank, making it difficult for the attackers to gain momentum as they thrust the ram. Bryk wanted to suspend the huge log from the canopy frame so men didn't have to labor uphill to carry it forward. Ropes would provide the power to lever it back and forth.

Covering the end of the ram with metal, if they'd had enough to feed the forge, would have increased its efficiency.

However, Hrolf was impatient to test it out before these embellishments were complete. All it took was a few sacks of sawdust, followed by burning hot sand dropped on the winded warriors to force a retreat just as the first crack splintered the massive door.

"The Franks didn't even need the grappling hooks they whittled overhead," Hrolf yelled in frustration before secluding himself inside his tent where he'd remained for several hours.

Bryk was tired. He hunkered down, his eyes drifting to the partially finished catapult. He wondered about the wisdom of spending more time and effort on it when distant dust clouds indicated troops massing. They should be conserving their strength, planning to defend against a relief army. It was unlikely Hrolf's wish to be inside the stubborn walls would come to fruition before they were attacked. A Viking's strength lay in raiding unfortified coastal towns and villages; there was much to be learned about penetrating impenetrable walls.

"We need to know the enemy's strength."

Bryk looked up from studying the ground. It was tempting to laugh out loud at the vision that confronted him, but he thought better of it. Hrolf had emerged from his tent, face so red and hair so tangled he looked like a snow capped beetroot.

He'd expected to be harangued about the shortcomings of the siege engine, but his chieftain launched into a proposal for scouting parties to spy on the enemy.

Stealthily roving through perilous open countryside suddenly seemed more appealing than spending another day sweating over the cursed catapult. He stood. "I'll go. Give me Alfred, and Sven Yngre."

Hrolf thrust out his bearded chin, closed one eye and scratched his head, as if contemplating the suggestion. "Agreed. The sooner the better."

Within a half hour, the resourceful Sven had separated three horses from the pack rounded up during Hrolf's raids. Despite his first terrifying experience on horseback, the lad had become an accomplished rider. Alfred too had long experience with horses.

"We'll follow the river to begin with, then venture towards what looks to be a camp," he told them.

They nodded in agreement. It occurred to him that Alfred never questioned what he did. He hoped he wasn't leading his brother to his death, though he'd noticed a transformation of sorts, a growth in Alfred's confidence. He supposed exposure to constant danger would make a warrior of any farmer.

They rode slowly along the bank for an hour, always with a weather eye to the place they judged the enemy camp to be located. Bryk called a halt when he spied something odd on the opposite bank of the river. It looked familiar, and yet—

"Longboats," Sven rasped. "Two I'd say. Hacked to bits."

Dread washed over Bryk as they dismounted and crept stealthily closer to the pile of debris. Though the destruction was complete, there was no doubt in his mind these were Viking boats, from Møre.

"What are they doing here?" Alfred wondered out loud.

Bryk scanned the riverbank. " I don't know. Judging by the trampled ground, they were destroyed by Frankish soldiers, and their crews taken prisoner."

"But who was manning them?"

A snake curled itself around Bryk's bowels. "There's one person I can think of who would know we needed reinforcements and who had the courage to lead them here."

"Poppa," Alfred acknowledged. "But only thralls were left in Rouen, apart from the garrison. She wouldn't leave the town unprotected."

The certainty that Poppa of Bayeux was in enemy hands, or dead, made his heart bleed for Hrolf. If it was Cathryn—

They waded through thigh deep water to reach the ruined boats, gradually aware of a familiar odor. The flies led them to a body that could only be Padraig. He'd a hole in his back the size of a fist.

"They tore the arrow out," Alfred rasped.

Sven shrugged. "Can't waste arrows on a thrall."

"But do they know they've captured thralls?" Bryk mused aloud.

His fear for Poppa grew.

Then he caught sight of a small chest floating in the water, its lid torn off. He'd given it to Torstein years ago. His suspicion that Hrolf's concubine had led a band of thralls was probably well founded. Was the lad now in enemy hands? The prospect saddened him. He'd sworn to protect the thrall after his brother's death. It was a pity Torstein had been born into slavery. In different circumstances Bryk, and he suspected Alfred, would have been proud to call the boy nephew.

As if his thoughts conjured him, Torstein sauntered out of the forest, accompanied by about a dozen men.

Bryk's spirits lifted as he slapped him on the back. "I was thinking what a resourceful fellow you are, and now you've proven it. What has gone on here? Have they taken Poppa?"

Torstein avoided his gaze. "*Ja*. And my mistress." He fell to his knees, head bowed. "I tried to protect her, but they were too many. I thought it best to flee to fight another day. We followed them to their camp, but I returned here. I knew you would come."

Bryk hardly heard a word he said. His heart was drumming too loudly in his ears.

IN ENEMY HANDS

"It's a large force with many horses," Torstein informed his master as they scrambled on their bellies up a slight rise, having left the horses with the remaining thralls near the river. "More than five score slaves have been herded together in the sun for hours with no food or water.

"There are few sentries. I think the Franks believe they have taken care of the problem of reinforcements and are preparing to attack our main army."

Bryk grasped Torstein's sleeve, clinging to a last hope he'd misunderstood. "Explain to me once more why Cathryn is here."

"She insisted on accompanying Poppa of Bayeux. She was killing your trees."

If his heart and gut weren't tied in knots he might have laughed. "What?"

Torstein looked him in the eye, a rarity for a slave. For a fleeting moment Bryk saw Gunnar's face. He'd never noticed the resemblance before.

"The apple trees. They do not respond to her care. She believes she is responsible for them withering. It made her sad. Also, I think she was unhappy living in the archbishop's house. They treated her badly, although the archbishop allowed her to work on his library, with Javune."

Bryk was astonished at Torstein's account. The thrall had never been known to utter more than a few words, and then only when spoken to. He even sounded like Gunnar. "Javune?" he asked, wondering what other unexpected events had taken place in his absence.

"He came with us from Rouen. He is one of the prisoners."

Bryk held his breath, trying to come to terms with the revelations. "Have they not discovered he's a Frank?"

"*Ja*, but Sprig is also here, and from what I could see I believe he discredited Javune."

Fury choked Bryk. "Sprig? He is under guard in Jumièges."

Torstein shook his head. "He is here. I have seen him. My mistress discovered he was in Rouen en route to some abbey in Neustria. He is the only one who could have told the relief army about our plan to bring reinforcements."

Bryk's blood was boiling. Not only was his wife a prisoner of the Franks she could fall prey once more to the depraved monk. "Neustria?"

"He is from there, according to Javune."

They continued their slow progress to the top of the rise, followed closely by Alfred and Sven. Torstein had warned they weren't far from the enemy and would have to keep their heads low. Nor could they linger long.

Bryk's eyes darted here and there, trying to ascertain the lay of the land. Soldiers, slaves, tents, two men seated in carved chairs.

Carved chairs?

"Don't mention the chairs to Hrolf. Might give him ideas," he rasped to Alfred and Sven. They chuckled in agreement. Even Torstein smiled weakly.

"Imagine the huge chair we'd have to lug everywhere for our chieftain," Alfred quipped.

"*Ja!*" Sven agreed. "And Poppa would insist on one for herself."

Bryk mused inwardly about the apparent need men felt to make light of the direst situations.

But his blood turned to ice when a black robed figure strode into view and stood by Burgundy's chair. There was no doubt in his mind it was Sprig.

"There stands the man who has betrayed the expedition to bring reinforcements," he rasped, relieved Cathryn and Poppa weren't among the thralls languishing in the intense heat. "The women must be in one of the tents," he said, refusing to consider the possibility his wife was already dead.

Moments later, only the restraining hands of his companions stopped him rushing from their hiding place, *stridsøkse* held high, ready to die in defense of Cathryn and Poppa as they strode from one of the tents. He choked down the battle cry threatening to erupt from his chest.

"Watching you being hacked to pieces won't help Cathryn," Alfred hissed.

Bryk calmed, reassured in part by his wife's posture. Despite the male attire, she walked like a queen about to accept the homage of her subjects, Poppa in tow. In contrast, Hrolf's concubine looked like a wary peasant. "She's not afraid," he whispered, knowing in his heart her faith in Saint Catherine's protection had given her courage.

"At least they're not being dragged before the nobles," Sven said.

The scene that unfolded was remarkable. Cathryn didn't wait for the noblemen to speak. She took the lead, and though Bryk was too far away to hear her words, it was evident she wasn't cowering in fear.

"They look surprised," Alfred said with a trace of a smile.

"She's scolding them," Bryk replied, his heart filling with pride.

Poppa appeared to remain silent throughout the interview. Cathryn continued to speak when the monk threw off his hood and shouted something at her. "Didn't even flinch," Bryk murmured.

"Richard of Burgundy doesn't look happy, but he seems more annoyed with the monk than with your wife," Alfred said.

When Cathryn finally stopped talking, the two noblemen exchanged a glance. The taller of the two said something to Cathryn who promptly turned on her heel and marched back to the tent.

"What a woman," Sven observed.

A ridiculous surge of jealousy boiled up in Bryk's gut. He'd have to speak to his wife about the tightness of the pants that showed off the tempting curve of her bottom. "*Ja*. But we must get them out of here. Sprig will keep on trying to discredit her. If he fails he'll plot some other means to exact revenge."

~~~

Throughout the interview with Richard of Burgundy Cathryn had chanted a mantra in the back of her mind.

Saint Catherine pray for me.

The saint had sustained her, and for that she was grateful, though her knees threatened to buckle as she and Poppa regained their tent.

However, an overwhelming sense of Bryk's closeness had cloaked her in a mantle of invincibility.

Burgundy admitted to admiring her courage, though he obviously thought her suggestion that Vikings and Franks might live together in peace and harmony was lunacy. Undeterred, she'd urged peace talks rather than war, explaining the Vikings had come to settle not to plunder and destroy. That notion had also fallen by the wayside, but at least she'd planted the seed in Burgundy's mind.

It had been unnerving keeping her composure in the face of Sprig's poisonous attacks, especially when he shouted for the mark of the devil to be scourged from Javune's back.

Poppa had eventually snapped out of her trance and almost growled at the monk. She had seconded without flinching Cathryn's avowal of faithfulness to her Viking husband.

It had been in Cathryn's mind to launch into a treatise of how tolerant the Vikings were in contrast to many Franks, but thought better of it. Nor did she deem it the appropriate moment to accuse Sprig.

She'd said enough and stayed true to her beliefs and her husband. Burgundy had agreed to spare Javune's life, though he'd been returned to the thralls' compound.

There was no guarantee anything she'd said would lead to peace, but at least they were still alive.

RESCUE

In the waning light, Bryk, Alfred and Sven sat in grass burned brown by the summer sun, discussing various ideas for the rescue, but every option seemed doomed to failure. Bryk was getting discouraged. The silence stretched into long minutes.

"I have a plan," Torstein said with unusual authority, causing everyone to glance up at him sharply.

He came to his feet. "They've forced some of the thralls to dig latrines and chop wood for the fires. When they start work on the morrow, Sven and I will be among them, but we'll be armed."

Bryk stood quickly. "As will I."

Torstein shook his head. "Your pardon, Master, but you are too big, and you don't look like a slave. We will join the prisoners under cover of darkness. The Franks won't notice two more men."

Bryk rubbed his chin. "Pity we don't have more weapons."

"They loosen the bonds so the men can dig. And I do have a few surprises." He shrugged the haversack off his back that he always carried and opened it. Inside lay a dozen daggers packed on top of his one spare tunic. "This should be enough to cause some confusion. They're from the other escaped thralls we left at the river."

Sven seemed anxious to add something. "Remember how we stampeded the horses in Jumièges. Mayhap—"

Bryk smiled.

Alfred grinned. "And while the Franks are dealing with the revolt and the horses, we'll steal into camp and rescue the women."

"Exactly," Torstein said. "But we won't start our disturbance until we're near the latrines. That way we'll draw more guards away from the women's tent."

Bryk put a hand on Torstein's shoulder, something he couldn't recall doing before. It was on the tip of his tongue to admit the resemblance to Gunnar, but all he could manage was, "I'm proud of you, lad."

~~~

Cathryn supposed she must have dozed during the long night. Poppa seemed to have slept soundly. Perhaps compared with being carried off by a Viking marauder who has just killed your father this perilous situation seemed more manageable to a woman born into the Frankish nobility.

Cathryn was sustained only by the firm belief that her patron saint would strengthen and protect her. And she believed Catherine of Alexandria also watched over Bryk.

The thralls packed together had been treated like dogs. She suspected some had died in the extreme heat without water and food. She felt shame for her countrymen. The moans of distress from the beleaguered slaves touched her heart. Javune was among them—a young man with no experience of physical hardship.

Poppa sat up abruptly. "Listen."

Cathryn had learned to respect her companion's ability to hear sounds no one else could. She strained to listen, but only the faint nickering of horses, distant male voices and the droning snore of the solitary guard outside their tent came to her ears. "I can't hear anything."

"The thralls have fallen silent."

Cathryn stopped breathing. Had the Franks grown tired of the wailing and cut their captives' throats? "What does it mean?" she whispered, deafened by her own heartbeat.

"It means they are either dead, or they have hope."

"They can't all be dead. Surely we'd have heard something if every one of them had been killed."

Poppa arched a brow. "Then it's hope that has caused them to silence their despair."

"What could have given them hope?"

But she knew the answer.

"Torstein."

Poppa nodded, coming to her feet. "We must be ready."

Cathryn had difficulty making her legs work. Hope at the moment of greatest despair was a powerful force that made her tremble from head to toe. She accepted the hand Poppa offered.

"You are a person of great faith and courage, Cathryn. I admire that in a woman. Your bravery has kept us alive."

She was about to reply when a commotion erupted outside. Men were running, shouting in Norse and the Frankish tongue. The sleeping guard cursed, having apparently toppled off his stool, startled by the din. Whinnying horses galloped by close to the tent. More shouting. Screams.

They clung together, expecting the guard to rush into the tent. They became alarmed when the pandemonium seemed to fade into the distance. Poppa peeped through the flap. "They've set fire to some of the bigger tents and pavilions. There are panicked horses running everywhere."

She and Cathryn whirled around when the back of their tent was suddenly torn asunder and Bryk's massive shoulders appeared as he strode through the rent.

Cathryn tried to form his name, but sound refused to emerge from her parched throat.

It dawned on her the man with Bryk was Alfred. Her brother-by-marriage bowed to Poppa and held out his hand. "We don't have much time."

Hrolf's concubine had stepped out of the tent before Cathryn could blink, but her feet seemed to be fixed to the dusty earth. Bryk scooped her up. "*Kom*, Cathryn," he rumbled. She melted into him, giving thanks to her patron saint for what might be the last opportunity to feel the warmth of his solid body and the strength of his arms.

~~~

Bryk set his wife on her feet and they ran and ran, his heart in turmoil knowing there was no safe place to take her. In the predawn darkness, he was reasonably confident they were heading in the right direction for the main Viking camp at Chartres. It was their only hope.

His lungs were on fire, his legs cramped. A sharp pain knifed into his side. He wondered how Cathryn was able to keep up with him. Good thing she was wearing male attire.

Suddenly she let go of his hand and fell to her knees, one hand braced against a tree trunk, gasping for breath.

Bryk went down on one knee. "Climb on my back," he ordered.

He sensed it was on the tip of her tongue to refuse, but it was evident she could go no further. She obeyed, her arms clinging to his neck as he carried her through forests, across parched fields and finally to the river.

He'd lost sight of Alfred and Poppa in the course of their flight and was relieved when his brother staggered out of the trees, Hrolf's concubine on his back. Even in this ungainly situation, the Frankish woman managed to look dignified.

He sank to his knees on the grassy bank and eased Cathryn to the ground. Whimpering, she refused to let go. He came to his feet and pressed her body to his, relishing the feel of her soft curves, but perturbed by the trembling that shook her. He stroked her hair. "Hush, hush. Safe now," he crooned, wishing it were true.

"Bryk," she murmured, her face nuzzled into his neck. "Bryk. I thought I would never see you again. I have killed your trees."

By Odin, how he loved this woman.

"I don't care about the trees," he replied, thankful the fire in his lungs had subsided. Now what to do with the fire in his loins? "You are my life, but we must keep moving."

As the first pink streaks of dawn lit the sky, he whistled softly. Men emerged from the trees like wraiths out of Hel, leading the horses they'd brought from Chartres.

Cathryn startled, but he reassured her. "Thralls," he explained. "Left with animals."

The relief on her tear-smudged face when she recognized some of the slaves touched his heart. He doubted she could have continued much further on foot.

The thralls were careful not to offend him but it was evident from their rare smiles they were glad to see her.

Because she treats them like free men.

They were more wary of Poppa, but Alfred exhibited no such caution as he hoisted Hrolf's concubine onto his horse and mounted behind her. She must be exhausted yet she kept her spine rigid.

Bryk mounted his horse and held out his hand to his wife. Their gazes locked. He was amazed to see no fear in her eyes. "We must leave here, though there is no safe place to take you," he admitted reluctantly.

"You are my refuge, husband," she said as she accepted his hand and mounted behind him. "Saint Catherine will protect us."

As he turned the horse south, he couldn't resist. "And Freyja."

She giggled, leaning against his back, her arms around his waist. "And Freyja."

It occurred to him as they made their escape that he'd never been in greater danger, yet he'd never been more content.

CALM BEFORE THE STORM

Bryk had never known Hrolf to allow his deepest emotions to show. He suspected that even the chieftain's angry outbursts were carefully planned for effect.

But when Alfred delivered Poppa into Hrolf's arms, the old warrior clung to her, raining kisses on her dirty face, cooing words of endearment. She sagged against him. He nodded a word of thanks to Alfred, then lifted her and carried her off to his tent, a giant bearing a tiny limp doll.

Cathryn had dozed against Bryk's back once it became evident they weren't being pursued, but the excitement of their arrival roused her. He dismounted carefully and put a hand on her leather-clad thigh, kneading his fingers gently into her flesh. "I like, but prefer dress."

Eyes flashing, she grinned at him. "I didn't bring a dress with me."

He laughed and put his hands on her waist. She gripped his shoulders as he lifted her from the horse. They clung together, her head on his chest. "*Kom* to my tent. I take care of you."

He noticed as they made their way arm in arm to the canvas shelter that no work had been done on the catapult. It was of no importance. With what he had to tell Hrolf about the relief army, there was no time left to continue a siege in any case.

He led his wife into his tent. "Not comfortable," he said, indicating his meager bedroll. "But you rest."

She smiled weakly, exhaustion etched on her lovely face. "If you rest with me," she said hoarsely.

The siege was lost, the catapult a waste of time and effort. The relief army was unlikely to launch an attack immediately after the fiasco of the prisoner revolt. It would take them a while to round up their horses. Hrolf wouldn't appreciate being bothered about defense strategy.

What else was there to do but lie abed all day with his beautiful wife? It might be his last opportunity before he was called to Valhalla. "*Ja!*" he replied, fiddling with the laces of Cathryn's leggings. "Good idea."

She yawned, stretching her arms above her head. "I'm too tired to take off my clothes."

He grinned. "Don't worry. I help with that."

~~~

Once Cathryn was naked, Bryk fetched water from the river and bathed her lovingly, apologizing he had only his calloused hands to cleanse her. The cool water and his gentle touch were like a balm to her soul. Though they faced almost certain death on the morrow, she'd never felt safer or more loved. Had Saint Catherine experienced this calm acceptance of the inevitable in the face of the Breaking Wheel? She'd miraculously destroyed the instrument of torture. Would they be granted their own miracle?

Scarcely able to keep her eyes open, she touched his shoulder. "Take off your clothes. Let me wash you."

He stripped quickly. She grimaced at the evidence of the hardships he'd endured during the siege. "You're bruised," she whispered, kissing the livid welt under his ribs. "And burned," she added, touching her fingertips to the raised red marks on his arms.

"Your touch makes better," he rasped.

She glanced at the evidence of interest stirring at his groin and smiled. "Later I'll make you feel even better, but for now, lie down and I'll cleanse you."

He obeyed. She dipped her hands in the cold water and smoothed them over his bronzed skin. "You've been working in the sun without a shirt," she murmured, admiring the play of his muscles as he responded to her touch.

"Catapult, battering ram, *Sambuca*, all waste of time," he replied, the back of his hand hiding the frown she suspected creased his forehead.

His obvious disappointment in the failure of the siege tore at her heart. He was a gentle man forced to fight for a piece of land to call his own. Francia was an enormous and fertile country. The unfairness of it rankled.

When she had washed the dust from his body, she bade him stand in the bucket. "Easiest way to clean your big feet," she teased.

He laughed, dipped one foot in, then the other. Suddenly, he grabbed her and drew her down to the bedroll. "Lie with me, Cathryn," he growled.

She sensed his exhaustion, but also his need for her. "Lay back," she whispered, coming to her knees between his legs. She circled the base of his shaft with her hand and leaned over to take him into her mouth.

"Cathryn," he rasped, smoothing her hair back behind her ear as she sucked him into the back of her throat in the rhythmic way she knew he loved. He closed his eyes. "I am in Valhalla already."

The skin of his thighs warmed. His breathing became labored. He tightened his grip on her hair. He moaned when she cupped his sack. She recognized the signs. The precious seed would soon erupt from his body, and she wanted it inside her.

His eyes widened when she suddenly stopped her ministrations and turned her back on him to straddle his hips. He groaned when she lowered herself onto his shaft, gripping his thighs. His fullness always filled her, but in this new position he possessed her completely.

"I'm home," he groaned.

"Welcome," she whispered.

"Ride me," he rumbled, clamping his hands on her hips.

She did just that, relishing the control as she raised then lowered her body on him, over and over.

He put a warm hand on her birthmark and slapped her gently. "*Jordbær*," he croaked. "My juicy strawberry."

A few more strokes and he cried out his release as the familiar heat of their joining flooded her body and peace filled her heart.

They clung together as he gradually softened. The sun climbed higher in the sky. She felt contentedly sticky, inhaling her husband's scent and listening to his soft snores as he dozed.

She admired his strong legs when he got up briefly and prowled around swatting at pesky bluebottles with his shirt. She laughed at his cry of triumph when he finally vanquished the last one. "My conqueror," she quipped.

On the morrow her soul might wing its way to heaven, but heaven was here on earth when Bryk came back to bed, knelt between her legs and licked her most intimate place. "Your turn now," he teased.

THE BATTLE

July 20, 911 AD, near Chartres, Francia

"The relief army is camped to the southwest of the city," Bryk reported to Hrolf at the gathering of the Viking captains the following day. "There are Franks, Burgundians, and men from Aquitaine."

He didn't want to add that it was a formidable force they faced. Their enemies had joined forces and their backs were to the walls of Chartres. Hrolf's stern expression betrayed that he already knew it. The presence of Poppa and Cathryn made matters worse. Bryk had considered suggesting they surrender to the Bishop of Chartres before the fighting began, but Hrolf would never agree.

He'd also thought of flight down the Eure, but there weren't enough seaworthy longboats left for everyone, and where would they go? Burgundy and Neustria would pursue them relentlessly.

At least he'd been able to secrete Cathryn and Poppa in one of the longboats, away from the action, with instructions to seek refuge in Chartres and beg for mercy if all was lost.

He'd silenced his wife's objections with a gentle kiss, wiping away her tears with his thumb. He'd given her a dagger and suspected neither she nor Poppa would surrender willingly.

Bryk drew his own dagger and crouched, using the point of the weapon to draw three circles in the sandy soil, trying to recall what he'd seen in the brief glimpse he'd had of the encampment. "Duke Richard has split his forces into three groups. Aquitainians camped here."

Hrolf nodded, stroking his beard, his long legs braced.

"Robert the Margrave is in the center with his Neustrians."

Hrolf remained silent.

"The Burgundians are massed on the other flank."

Hrolf coughed up phlegm and spat at the spot Bryk had pointed to. "We will form up in a half circle and surround them."

Bryk nodded his agreement. He too thought taking the offensive was their only hope. They'd be slaughtered pinned against the walls of the town. But Hrolf's next command took him by surprise. "I will lead one end of the charge. Bryk Kriger will lead the other."

The word was passed and the Vikings quickly took up familiar positions. The dust kicked up by the horses of the Frankish army blossomed like a cloud on the horizon. Bryk wished he had Fisk beneath him.

"They're coming," Hrolf shouted as the dust cloud moved closer. "Wait for my signal."

Bryk shifted his *stridsøkse* to his left hand and wiped the sweat from his right palm on his padded pants, then drew his sword. He could wield an axe with his weaker hand, and the sword hefted better in the right.

The weather was hot and humid, the sun blazing down—nothing like summer in Møre—and he was sweating under the mail shirt and his heavy helmet. The wooden shield strapped to his back felt like a lead weight.

He didn't worry overmuch about it. Once the battle began the icy chill of fear would quickly take hold and he'd be flying like a bird, striking down any who might challenge him.

He didn't fear death. He had earned a place in either Odin's Valhalla or Freyja's Fólkvangr and was sure the Valkyries would carry him to one of the gods' feasting halls. If he had a choice—

When Duke Richard's army galloped into sight, yelling their battle cry, he abandoned all thoughts of the goddess of fertility and offered a quick entreaty to Saint Catherine—just in case.

Hrolf clenched his jaw, his steely gaze fixed on the advancing horde. Bryk was initially surprised how few of the enemy were actually mounted. Evidently they'd had trouble rounding up their frenzied mounts. That evened the game somewhat. He hadn't relished crippling horses to unseat their riders.

Hrolf raised his axe. "*Aaaangrrrrrep!*" he bellowed, leading the charge on the left flank. Bryk yelled his own war cry and set the right flank in motion.

There was a momentary but noticeable lull in the shouting coming from the Frankish side. The sight of a white-haired bearded giant rushing toward them, armed with a menacing axe bigger than most men, would be enough to make any soldier's throat constrict, not to mention his sphincter muscles.

Bryk smiled inwardly, but grimly hoped he wouldn't soil himself. He'd seen enough death to be aware of what happened to a man's bowels. He'd been in many skirmishes, but this was different. His thoughts went to Møre, to Myldryd and his ancestors buried far away.

They had begun this odyssey in the hope of securing land for a new life. Now it seemed all might be lost. But he would fight with honor for what he came for, even to the death, though he regretted with all his heart that Cathryn would be left alone—again.

With well practiced discipline the Viking flanks surged as the center held back. Bryk loped along steadily, wanting to keep up with Hrolf's long strides, but needing to conserve his strength. He'd soon need every ounce of it.

~~~

The two sides came together in an enormous cloud of choking dust. Unsure of his targets, Bryk swung his sword and axe, satisfied when metal met flesh and his enemies fell at his feet. He strode over bodies, bellowing a war cry. All around him men died, some screaming as limbs were hacked off and blood flowed, others slipping silently into death without a whimper.

The dust cleared for a moment. He squinted into the melee, astonished to see Alfred bring down a Frankish soldier. His brother had somehow acquired a sword and shield and obviously knew how to handle them. They grinned at each other like naughty boys, but then the dust obscured his vision and he moved on, hacking and slashing and praying.

For a while it seemed the Franks were giving ground. They suddenly seemed preoccupied with something happening behind them.

Bryk came close to whooping with glee when he caught sight of Torstein leading a horde of Viking slaves against the Franks' rear guard. His spirits lifted when the enemy fell back further.

But his joy was short-lived. He swiveled his head as the heavy gates of Chartres creaked open, the din audible even over the clash of battle. He blinked twice, fearing he was hallucinating.

The Bishop of Chartres, crowned with his episcopal mitre as though about to celebrate mass, and holding high a cross, strode forth from inside the walls followed by the clergy and townsfolk armed with spears and swords. They rushed forward, lashing the backs of the Vikings.

The battle raged on. Bryk lost all sense of time. His biceps ached and he could barely lift his weapons. He'd lost his shield some time ago and was covered in blood. He was sure his helmet must be battered beyond recognition. Thirst raged in his throat, grit scoured his eyeballs every time he blinked. But he was alive—for the moment.

He inhaled deeply, preparing to enter the fray again when he saw something he never thought to see in his lifetime.

Hrolf stood on the other flank, waving a white flag.

SURRENDER

B ryk swayed and had to jam his sword into the dry ground and lean on it lest he fall over. Duke Richard called a halt to the battle. It took time for the Vikings to realize their chieftain had surrendered and for the Frankish soldiers to become aware of their leader's orders.

Bryk fell to his knees, still leaning on the sword while minor skirmishes continued around him. The axe fell from his cramped hand. If he died in the next few minutes, so be it. He was a dead man anyway. Everything he had fought for crumbled at the sight of Hrolf surrendering to Burgundy. His dream of tending his apple trees while watching Cathryn's belly grow round with his child was swept away. He wondered if he had enough strength left to at least get to the longboat to defend her against violation.

He struggled to his feet, but staggered when he was shoved from behind. He understood enough of the Frankish tongue to know he was being ordered to move towards the hill where Hrolf stood. A Frank picked up his axe and brandished it under his nose. Did the fool not realize Bryk could snap him like a twig?

But what further need did he have for the axe, or the sword? He allowed himself to be herded together with those of his battered countrymen who'd survived. He was surprised by how many still lived, but worried that he didn't see Alfred among them, or Torstein. It gladdened his heart to catch sight of Sven Yngre, bloodied and bruised, but still alive, leaning on an apparently unscathed Javune. Though what future did the young men have now?

As they limped away, it struck him there was something about Javune he should be paying attention to, but whatever it was eluded his befuddled brain.

The Vikings stood before Richard of Burgundy, but it was Hrolf who addressed them.

"We have come to terms with Duke Richard and Margrave Robert and have agreed to surrender. We will be allowed to remain on this hill to tend our wounded and bury our dead. In exchange we have agreed to hand over good faith hostages."

A terrible foreboding crept into Bryk's heart. He glanced at the leader of the Franks, knowing only too well whom the Burgundian had stipulated.

"Duke Richard has requested that my wife, Poppa of Bayeux, be one of the hostages, and Cathryn, wife of Bryk Kriger be the other."

Rage exploded in Bryk's chest as he leapt to his feet. *"Jamais!"* he spat at Burgundy in his own tongue.

Hrolf raised a hand, his lined face twisted in torment. "Calm yourself, brother. I have agreed."

~~~

The Vikings were not allowed to leave the hill, but nuns and monks from Chartres gradually brought first the wounded, then the dead from the field.

Bryk eventually located Alfred who sported a purple goose egg on his forehead, and Torstein who showed off the finger severed from his bandaged left hand with great pride to anyone who might listen.

Reassured the remnants of his family were safe, he hastened to find Hrolf. He was about to harangue his chieftain about the decision to sacrifice Cathryn and Poppa when their attention was drawn to a dust cloud to the north.

"More Franks," Hrolf spat. "They're a little late."

Within an hour, a large group of infantrymen led by a knight on horseback had joined Richard's camp. From their position on the hill, it was easy to see that the recently arrived knight and the Duke were arguing. From time to time the newcomer looked back at the hill.

"Whoever he is, he wants to attack us," Hrolf rumbled. "He's come late to the party and is angry he missed the action."

"Will Richard honor the arrangement?" Bryk asked, knowing in his heart the Duke would likely capitulate and assist a further attack.

"We must get to the longboats," Hrolf said. "At least there we can offer a defense."

Suddenly, the newcomer wheeled his horse to face them and ordered his men up the hill. The Vikings had only their bare hands to defend themselves. It would be a massacre. As the infantrymen began the climb, Duke Richard rode to the base of the hill, shouting at the top of his lungs.

The newcomer glared up at the Vikings, then ordered his men to retreat.

Hrolf spat. "Poitou. That's the name Burgundy yelled. He'll sleep on it then try again on the morrow. We must act tonight."

~~~

Cathryn and Poppa crouched in the trees downriver from the longboats and watched the handful of Frankish soldiers search every one of them, and then turn their attention to the abandoned camp, eventually leaving with a handful of bleating sheep from the pens.

"They are looking for us," Poppa whispered. "The battle has not gone in our favor."

They'd spent hours on their knees praying for a victory. Now their husbands were probably dead and they were alone in enemy territory.

Despair threatened to overwhelm Cathryn. Perhaps she was being punished for living in sin with a pagan. She closed her eyes, conjuring an image of her beloved. There was no evil in him. Loving such a man couldn't be sinful. "Saint Catherine has abandoned us," she murmured hoarsely.

"There were perhaps moments when she believed God had abandoned her," Poppa replied softly. "I refuse to give up hope. Hrolf believed we would settle and prosper in this land. I still have faith."

They remained hidden until well after nightfall. Cathryn's legs were so cramped she feared she'd be unable to stand. She was about to struggle to her feet to attend to the call of nature when an eerie, mournful wail splintered the silence.

Poppa got up quickly and grasped Cathryn's arm. "It's a Viking horn."

They crept stealthily out of the forest, their hopes lifting as more and more horns added to the cacophony.

They had almost reached the longboats when strong arms grabbed them from behind.

"Aha!" a male voice declared.

THE RUSE

The Franks evidently believed the horns that most Vikings wore slung across their bodies weren't dangerous. Bryk hoped that might be the key to their escape.

They'd waited until well after nightfall to put their plan into effect. Those who were able crept into the Frankish encampment, filled their lungs with air, then blew their horns.

The result was predictable. The sleeping Franks jumped to the conclusion they were under attack and scattered in all directions.

"Good of them to leave us the stretchers," Hrolf quipped as the Vikings carried their wounded down the hill and headed to the boats under cover of darkness.

Bryk clung to the hope Cathryn hadn't been captured, but there was no sign of the women once they arrived.

There was no time to search for them, however, until the second part of the plan had been put into place, and Bryk breathed a sigh of relief that the livestock were still in the pens. Some of the thralls had already unearthed weapons hidden on board and begun the slaughter. It went against all his farming instincts to kill animals for anything but food and self-preservation. He reasoned that the latter was the case here.

~~~

"We meet again, Cathryn, wife of Bryk," Richard of Burgundy quipped, lounging in his ornate chair in the dimly lit tent.

Cathryn was tempted to voice her opinion of a man who had a carved chair lugged around the countryside, but this wasn't the time. Exhaustion and fear had stolen her wits.

She had no idea what had happened to Poppa. They'd been separated immediately upon being brought into the Frankish camp. She decided to act as though Richard was Emperor Maxentius and she Catherine of Alexandria.

"I will not yield," she insisted, head held high.

Burgundy frowned. "Yield to what?" he asked. "No one here will molest you."

She hesitated, but her tormentor had to be exposed or she might find herself once more at his mercy. "There is one among you who has already tried to rape me."

He chewed his lower lip, eyeing her with suspicion. "Name him," he said, his voice edged with anger.

"Sprig."

He appeared startled. "The monk?"

She nodded.

Trust blossomed on his face. "He has already left to continue his journey to Vézelay, but he'll be dealt with. I loathe dishonorable men who attack women, especially a cleric—"

"Thank you," she breathed, relief flooding through her veins that he believed her. But she had to get the discussion back to the Vikings. "I will continue to suggest that peace talks will achieve more than bloodshed. Why can the Norsemen not be granted a portion of our country?"

Burgundy stroked his beard. "Charles the Senseless might say that notion is treasonous."

She opened her mouth to offer a retort but then realized he was smiling. "The King might believe calling him *Senseless* is treason," she replied.

The smile left his face. "Vikings are not known as peace loving people. If we give them a little, they might want a lot more."

Cathryn's thoughts went to Hrolf. Richard didn't know him, yet he'd summed up the Viking leader. "Most of them are like my husband. They are hard-working men who simply want a fertile piece of land on which to grow crops and raise a family. They would defend it to the death."

Richard leaned forward, gripping the arms of his chair, but the corners of his mouth still quirked upwards. "And what crop would your Viking grow?"

"Apples. He brought the seeds and rootstocks from Norway. Some that he planted in Rouen still live, though I managed to kill several."

Richard burst out laughing. "I hope your Viking knows what a priceless treasure he has in you."

She felt her face redden. "I am nothing, a foundling left on the threshold of a convent, but the Norsemen have a long and proud history and will contribute much to the prosperity and strength of Francia."

Burgundy frowned. "A foundling?"

She nodded, staring at her feet, feeling very uncomfortable in male attire.

The Duke's eyes wandered from her toes to the top of her head. "You are without doubt the most intelligent, the most courageous and the most beautiful foundling I've ever met."

Remember you are Catherine of Alexandria and even the best of men...

"But will you free the Vikings?"

Burgundy came to his feet slowly. "We'll have to see what King Charles says about the Vikings settling in Francia, but you are right, Cathryn. They are a resourceful people. They've already freed themselves."

PEACE

Hrolf strode into Bryk's tent, brandishing a parchment. "Charles the Senseless has come to his senses. He realizes we aren't going away. He has sent a message proposing a discussion of peace."

Bryk leapt to his feet, marveling at the favor the gods bestowed on a man who had lost an important battle, yet seemed to have won the war. The plan to build a barricade with the slaughtered animals had proven very effective the day after the flight from the hill. The Franks had regrouped and come in pursuit, but their horses were put off by the smell of blood and would not advance. Since then they'd been left unmolested, though the stench worsened with every passing day of intense heat. It seemed a stalemate had settled in.

In the sennight since the disappearance of Cathryn and Poppa, Bryk had fretted, cursed, drunk himself half blind with Hrolf, and prayed. The only moment of relief had been the arrival of a missive from Burgundy reaffirming that the women were his hostages, and that they were 'in good health.'

"The king awaits us by the river," Hrolf declared.

"Charles has arrived?" Bryk asked, fledgling hope burgeoning in his heart.

"Apparently," Hrolf replied impatiently.

They walked the half league to the meeting place, a small stream off the Eure. Backed by ranks of foot soldiers, the King, Richard and Robert sat atop their horses on the far bank. Behind them Bryk recognized Poitou. The hothead held the reins of two horses. Cathryn was mounted on one, Poppa on

155

the other. Bryk's head suddenly felt like he'd been drinking stale beer all night. His wife was clothed in fine raiment, her black hair adorned with a gold circlet. Who had given her these fine things? The answer was obvious. "Burgundy," he spat under his breath.

Dreadful suspicions entered his mind, but then he looked at Cathryn's face. Her gaze was for him alone. He recalled something Hrolf often said. *"The eyes of a maid tell true to whom her love she has given."*

He glanced again at Richard of Burgundy. Perhaps the man wasn't the monster he'd assumed.

Hrolf summoned Bryk to stand beside him.

Robert of Neustria cupped his hands to his mouth and shouted, "Poppa of Bayeux and Cathryn of Rouen have spoken of your desire to settle in these lands. The King asks what it is you want."

Cathryn of Rouen.

Bryk liked the sound of that.

Hrolf filled his lungs. "Let me and my people live in the land of the Franks," he bellowed back across the water. "We will make our home here, and become your vassals."

He turned to Bryk. "I can't see from this distance. Does he look angry?"

Bryk shaded his eyes. "Hard to tell, but he hasn't said anything to the others."

Hrolf nodded then turned back to the king. "I will take Rouen as my capital, and the land around it. In return we will defend the Seine from future attacks."

"He's discussing it," Bryk advised his chieftain moments later.

Richard of Burgundy called back. "You pledge to defend against other Viking attacks?"

Hrolf answered immediately. "It will be our land. We will defend it against any invader."

There was a long pause, then the King himself shouted. "You will not invade other lands in my kingdom."

It was not a question.

"Agreed."

The king shifted his weight in the saddle. "Becoming my vassal means that if I go to war you will be obliged to join my army and bring armed men—one thousand or more."

"Agreed."

"And will you forsake your pagan gods and worship the One True God?"

To Bryk's surprise, his chieftain didn't hesitate for a moment. "All my people will convert to the Christian God."

A calm Bryk had never known stole into his heart. He would become an adherent of Cathryn's faith openly and without fear. They could marry. Cathryn's broad smile across the stream fired his blood further.

"We will cede to you the land between the River Epte and the sea—" the king declared,

Hrolf nodded.

"—and Flandres."

Hrolf pouted. "Too marshy."

Bryk held his breath.

The king scowled. "Bretagne, then."

Hrolf chuckled. "Charles the Senseless isn't so senseless after all. The Franks have never been able to conquer the Bretons, now he wants me to do it. This will be a start, my friend. There's a lot of good land we must cross to get to Bretagne. It can be ours for the taking if we're patient."

Suddenly he became serious. "Before we left Møre, I had a vision," he confided. "I foresaw my baptism into the religion of the White Christ and peoples of many races united under my rule."

Bryk had long suspected his chieftain's dreams of power and glory, but was astonished to hear the words uttered out loud. What of the claims that Odin had revealed the future?

Hrolf addressed the king. "We agree, provided that our women are returned to us and our territory be known as *Terra Normannorum*." He chuckled again. "That bit of Latin should impress him."

Land of the Northmen.

Bryk liked the sound of that too.

"There is one last condition," Burgundy shouted. "You must offer a token of homage. It is customary for vassals to kiss the foot of the king."

Fury darkened Hrolf's face. "Never," he hissed between gritted teeth, "will I bend my knee before any man, and no man's foot will I kiss."

In the ensuing silence Bryk sensed the dismay of the hundreds of men behind him. All they desired and had fought for was within their grasp, but Hrolf's pride would snatch it away. Bryk had dealt with pride before. "I will kiss the king's foot," he said.

Hrolf stared at him for long minutes, then shouted to the king. "My lieutenant will perform the act of homage."

Charles hesitated then nodded his approval.

Bryk waded across the stream. The king watched him down his long nose. Standing by the side of the horse, he feared what he was about to do might jeopardize the peace agreement. But he too was a proud Viking. He had to perform homage but make it palatable to his countrymen. He'd redeemed himself in their eyes in large measure, but perhaps after this the *skalds* would sing his praises once more.

He seized the king's foot and drew it up to his lips so quickly, Charles narrowly averted falling from his horse, saved only by the quick thinking of Burgundy. Laughter broke out among the Vikings; loudest of all boomed Hrolf's bellow.

Charles glared. Bryk strode over to Poitou, took the reins of both horses, mounted behind his wife and urged the horse back across the stream, Poppa's mount in tow.

Hrolf slapped Bryk's horse on the rump as he strode towards Poppa. "Well done, brother," he shouted, as he helped his wife from her mount. "He's angry, but the peace will hold. And we've gained two fine horses. One for you, one for me."

Bryk turned the horse towards the camp, tightening his arms around his beloved. He nibbled her ear. "You have turned out to be a courageous diplomat, my love," he murmured in his own language, not expecting she would understand.

She leaned back against him and to his surprise replied in Norse. "Thanks to me, Hrolf will have no choice but to reward you handsomely, husband. I saved his wife and rescued his dreams of glory."

OATHS

Afortnight later, Bryk and Cathryn stood hand in hand in Chartres cathedral. He thought it best not to mention it was the first time he'd ever been in a Christian church and not had looting on his mind.

King Charles, Richard, Duke of Burgundy, and Robert, Margrave of Neustria, local magnates, bishops and abbots, bound themselves by the oath of the Catholic faith to Hrolf, who stood before them, Poppa at his side.

They swore by their lives and their bodies and by the honor of the entire kingdom that he might hold the land and transmit it to his heirs from generation to generation throughout all time to come.

"It's a miracle," Bryk whispered.

Cathryn smiled. "If you pray and have faith—"

Bryk squeezed her hand as the dignitaries trooped out of the cathedral. "The King looks content."

Cathryn giggled. "Not nearly as content as Hrolf, and you'd think Poppa had been crowned Queen of all Francia."

Bryk inhaled the fresh air once they exited the church. "Now we can return to Rouen and see to my trees."

Cathryn cringed. "You won't be happy."

~~~

It came as a pleasant surprise to discover that many of Bryk's trees had not only survived but flourished. The maidservant who'd welcomed them back to the Archbishop's house in Rouen as if they were her long lost children explained. "His Grace instructed his gardener to take care of them."

"Evidently, we are acceptable now," Cathryn said to Bryk in his language, all the while smiling at the maid who had previously shunned her.

"Of course," he replied. "Norsemen hold the power here now. Anyone who fails to respect you will answer to me."

Though the woman didn't speak his language, she obviously understood his tone and the look in his eye. She smoothed back an errant curl, her gaze fixed on her feet. "His Grace has requested you meet him in his office." She bobbed a curtsey and left.

Cathryn burst out laughing. "I've never been curtseyed to before!"

Bryk frowned. "What does he want, I wonder?"

"I don't know. He was uncomfortably interested in everything about me before I left with Poppa."

They made their way to the small chamber at the other end of the house. The Archbishop hadn't arrived, but Cathryn was startled to see Javune seated in an ornate chair, looking nervous and unsure.

He leapt to his feet when they entered. "Cathryn," he exclaimed. "What are you doing here?"

"I was about to ask you the same thing," she replied.

He shrugged. "I was summoned, no doubt to be punished for running away. I expect to be sent off to some remote monastery."

"But no robe," Bryk said. "You wear ordinary clothes."

Before he could reply, Archbishop Franco swooped in, greeting them all with uncharacteristic good cheer and insisting they sit down. "We're just waiting for one more person, then we'll begin," he said.

He paced back and forth in a room too small for such an activity, hands clasped behind his back. After two or three uncomfortable minutes, the door creaked open. Cathryn leapt to her feet to embrace the unexpected visitor. "Ekaterina!" she exclaimed.

~~~

As the old nun embraced him, a twinkle in her eye, Bryk was still preoccupied with Javune's outfit. Obviously some Viking, possibly Torstein, had given him castoffs, but that wasn't what bothered him.

The last time he'd seen Javune after the defeat at Chartres, the young man had been stripped to the waist, and something about that had struck him as odd. He'd been too exhausted and defeated to think on it then, but he closed his eyes and tried to conjure the scene. Javune and Torstein were limping away. He'd been relieved they hadn't suffered any wounds, although Javune had a mark on his back that looked like—

He blinked his eyes wide open. "*Jordbær*," he exclaimed.

"Your pardon?" the Archbishop asked.

Cathryn's eyes filled with alarm as she glanced from him to Javune and back.

She knows.

Javune frowned nervously.

Ekaterina winked.

The Archbishop bade everyone regain their seats. He cleared his throat. "What I have to tell you will not be easy for me to say, nor for you to hear."

Bryk glanced at Cathryn. The courageous woman who'd helped his countrymen establish a claim to vast tracts of Francia suddenly looked like a frightened child. He swore under his breath to kill the cleric with his bare hands if anything that happened in the next few minutes resulted in harm to his wife.

"Many years ago, twenty to be exact, my brother, Bernardus, drowned in the Seine."

Bryk's heart lurched, his thoughts going to his brother whose body had never been recovered from the North Sea.

Javune still frowned.

Ekaterina's eyes were closed but Bryk knew she wasn't asleep.

Cathryn's mouth had fallen open.

Franco cleared his throat again. "His wife, Faregilda, was with child. The shock of my brother's death was so great, she took to her bed and never left it. She died in childbirth."

Javune scratched his scalp, obviously having no idea what was coming next, but Bryk knew.

Ekaterina peeled open one eye, her face reddening as an unpleasant odor permeated the air. "Pardon," she murmured.

Cathryn seemed to be holding her breath, but Bryk doubted it was because of the reek of flatulence.

Franco fidgeted with the sleeve of his cassock. "I was a young cleric, recently ordained. Our parents were dead. We had no siblings. At the time it seemed I had no option but to entrust my brother's offspring to the Church."

Cathryn gripped the arms of her chair and stared at the Archbishop. "You left me in a basket on the doorstep of the convent," she said hoarsely.

"You and your brother," Ekaterina said softly.

All eyes swiveled to the nun.

"I myself found the basket with two sleeping angels, a boy and a girl. Beautiful twins."

Javune's leg had begun to twitch.

Bryk took hold of Cathryn's hand. It was ice cold. He felt helpless to help her deal with this astounding news.

Ekaterina came to her feet. "When the boy turned one, the nuns decided he couldn't stay at the convent. He was given to a married couple who had tried unsuccessfully to have children of their own. The girl, my sweet Cathryn, stayed at the convent."

Cathryn turned to Ekaterina. "Did you know the Archbishop was my uncle?"

The nun shook her head. "I have suspicion only recently, when his Grace start to ask many questions, and when he directed me to accompany you to Jumièges."

Franco fell to his knees in front of Cathryn. "Forgive me. I was young. But you are my flesh and blood and I have followed your progress. I made sure you lacked nothing. I encouraged

Mater Silvia to take you under her wing. It was no hardship for her. She loved you. I wanted you to meet Javune."

Bryk wanted to kiss away the tears streaming down his wife's face. She had learned the identity of her parents, but so much had been taken away.

Javune jumped to his feet. "I don't understand what all this has to do with me," he said. "If you're going to send me off to a monastery, why do I have to sit and listen to this sad story?"

Cathryn took his hand. "Because you are my brother."

He stared at her for long moments then pulled his hand away. "No. It cannot be true. My parents have another child, my older brother."

Franco came to his feet. "It has taken some time to discover what happened to you, Javune. Ekaterina didn't know the name of the people who took you as their own, but she recalled the man had a large mole on his cheek."

Javune sucked in a breath.

"There is only one man in Rouen with such a mark on his face. Faroin Crochette."

Javune shook his head. "I don't understand."

"Shortly after you went to live with them, Faroin discovered his wife was with child. They've admitted to lying to you because they wanted their own flesh and blood child to inherit. Your stepbrother is actually younger than you are.

"As you grew to manhood, they feared you might discover the truth, so they sent you to a monastery."

Javune stared at the cleric. "Faroin Crochette is not my father?"

Franco shook his head. "We mustn't judge them. What they did was wrong, but—"

Fury darkened Javune's face. "There is no proof of any of this."

"You have a strawberry shaped birthmark on your lower back," Cathryn said softly. "I saw it when Burgundy was questioning you."

"Of what consequence is that?" Javune retorted.

"Cathryn has the same mark," Bryk replied, when it became obvious his wife couldn't speak.

"You both inherited that mark from my brother. He and I inherited it from our father," Archbishop Franco explained.

"*Da!*" Ekaterina exclaimed, slapping her rump. "On the bottom."

The Archbishop's face reddened as he cleared his throat. "Yes, well—"

Javune raked a hand through his hair, his eyes darting from one person to the next. Then his gaze settled on Cathryn. "You are my sister," he rasped.

Bryk's heart filled with joy for his wife when she rose from her seat and embraced her brother. They clung together for long minutes.

"*Da!*" Ekaterina declared again.

~~~

Cathryn's emotions were all at sea. In the space of ten minutes she'd discovered a brother, an uncle, and the names and fates of her parents. She was no longer a nameless foundling.

But joy was tinged with sadness for the wrongs perpetuated.

However, what was the point of bitterness when she had so much to be happy about? She broke away from Javune and faced Franco. "I never thought to call an Archbishop *oncle*," she said with a smile.

He opened his arms and she and Javune went willingly.

"I was frantic with worry when you both disappeared with the Vikings," he said, his voice catching in his throat. "When you first entered into a Danish marriage with Bryk, Cathryn, I was furious, but I realized when I got to know him a little better he was a noble and trustworthy man.

"I wanted him to know he had married a woman of noble birth."

Bryk bristled. "I don't need you to tell me this," he protested.

"I know," Franco admitted. "But it is only right that you both receive the inheritance my brother left. It's several hundred *livres*. I swear in my brother's name neither of you will lack for anything."

Cathryn suspected from the scowl on Bryk's face this would be a blow to his pride. "My husband provides well for me, *oncle*. My brother can have my share."

"Let me understand this," Javune said. "I don't have to go back to the monastery?"

Franco chuckled. "Only if you want to."

Javune winked at Cathryn and she knew exactly what he had in mind. "I know a young woman here in Rouen who will be only too glad to meet a wealthy, educated and handsome nobleman with blue eyes."

As Ekaterina opened her mouth to speak, a chorus of agreement sounded from everyone else in the chamber. "*Da!*" they exclaimed together.

The old nun laughed till tears ran down her wrinkled face, and her chortles of glee could still be heard after they'd all fled the room, unable to breathe.

BAPTISM

Rouen 912 AD

Bryk had expected his chieftain to be nervous, but he seemed at peace as he stood before Archbishop Franco in Rouen Cathedral. The cleric turned to Robert of Neustria. "Who is this man's godfather?"

"I am," Robert declared.

"And what name shall he receive as he is baptized into the new life of Christ?"

"Rollo," Robert replied in a booming voice that echoed in the rafters of the cathedral.

Franco dipped his thumb into the water he had blessed earlier and made a sign on Hrolf's forehead.

"It's the sign of our Savior's suffering," Cathryn whispered.

Bryk nodded, noting a tear trickling down Poppa's cheek as she stood beside her Viking, Vilhelm behind them. Rollo swore to honor God and cling to no other faith. Franco then blessed his marriage to Poppa.

The archbishop turned to address the hundreds of Vikings assembled to witness the historic event. "I understand there are some among you— "

Bryk clutched Cathryn's hand and stepped forward from the front of the crowd, unable to wait any longer to embrace his wife's faith. With Cathryn's help he'd practiced over and over the right words to say. "I am Bryk Gardbruker and I ask the

Lord God to cleanse me of my sins and accept me into baptism."

~~~

Cathryn didn't really hear most of the Latin ritual the Archbishop subsequently intoned for the hundreds who came forward to convert. Her heart was beating too loudly in her ears. Her gaze was for one man, her rover bold, the Viking who'd stolen her heart and brought her more pleasure and happiness than she'd ever believed possible. She fingered the copper amulet Bryk had given her after she'd told him she was with child. It was almost an exact replica of the one he wore, but the runic inscription was different. *When two hearts yearn for each other, the hotter the flame of love waxes.*

It had moved her to tears.

But his and Alfred's recognition of Torstein as their nephew after he'd granted the boy his freedom had overwhelmed her, especially when many of his fellow Vikings deemed it an incomprehensible and foolhardy decision.

Once outside the cathedral, Bryk took her in his arms. "By Odin, I feel like a new man, as though the regrets of the past have been swept away." He kissed her forehead. "And thanks be to Freyja for the little one growing in your belly. Now the Church has blessed his parents' marriage, he won't be a bastard."

Cathryn rolled her eyes, tempted to laugh. Expecting Bryk to abandon his Norse gods would be like asking him to stop breathing.

But her husband was right that life held promise. Rollo had given assurances of security to all those who wished to dwell in his country. He had divided the land among his followers, granting Bryk and Cathryn a handsome and fertile tract near the Seine, as well as a guarantee of more to come as their campaign against the Bretons continued and other lands fell under the control of the Norsemen.

Alfred and Hannelore had been given a swath of land adjacent to Bryk's.

Rollo had already begun the construction of many new buildings in Rouen and the rebuilding of ruined churches. Word had spread quickly that immigrants were welcome and more Norsemen had arrived, as well as Danes from Britain.

Rights and laws had been put into place and everyone understood people were expected to live peaceably together. Several thieves and murderers had already been hanged.

Repairs had begun on the town's walls and fortifications, Rollo reminding everyone, whether they wanted to listen or not, of the lessons learned at Chartres.

VIKING FACT AND FICTION

Sometimes truth is stranger than fiction.

D id Hrolf Ganger lead a band of Vikings to the valley of the Seine in the 10th century and eventually become Rollo, First Duke of Normandy? YES.
Did the Vikings attempt to seize Chartres? YES
Did a Viking lieutenant almost topple King Charles the Senseless from his horse when offering a sign of homage? YES, according to historians writing hundreds of years later.
Did the Vikings escape from a hill where they'd been cornered by creeping into the Frankish camp and blowing horns in the middle of the night? YES.
Did they build a barricade of slaughtered animals? YES.
Speaking of horns, did Viking helmets have horns? NO. This is a misconception perpetuated after Richard Wagner's costume designer, Carl Emil Doepler, created horned helmets for the first Bayreuth Festival performance of the opera *Der Ring des Nibelungen.*
Did Poppa of Bayeux exist? YES. She was the mother of Rollo's son, William Longsword (Vilhelm) who succeeded his father as Duke of Normandy.
Were the Normans who invaded England in 1066 AD descendants of Rollo and his Vikings? YES. William the Conqueror was a direct descendant of Rollo.

Did the Bishop of Chartres lead the citizens' march out of the town to attack the Vikings from the rear? YES. Wearing his mitre he held aloft a crucifix and a relic referred to as 'la chemise de la Vierge' (the Virgin's Chemise). It became a popular relic, which unfortunately was destroyed in a fire in 1194 AD.

Was Franco Archbishop of Rouen? YES. From 911 AD to 919 AD.

Did Franco have a brother named Bernardus who drowned in the Seine? HIGHLY UNLIKELY.

What happens next? Find out in Book Two of the Viking Roots Medieval Romance Saga, THE ROVER DEFIANT.

VIKING BREAD

The recipe is courtesy of the Royal British Columbia Museum and is based on an analysis of Viking Age bread found in Birka, Sweden.

About 150 grams barley flour (approx. 2/3 cup)
About 50 grams whole meal flour (approx. 1/4 cup)
2 tsp crushed flax seeds
About 100 ml water
2 tsp lard or butter
Pinch of salt

Work the ingredients together into a dough and knead. If the dough is too wet or hard, add flour or water. Let the dough rest cold for at least one hour, preferably longer. Shape the dough into flat cakes about half a centimeter thick. Bake them in a dry cast iron pan on the stove over medium heat, a few minutes on each side or in the oven at 150° Celsius (300° F) for 10-13 minutes.

THE AMULET

Through the fabric of his shirt, Bryk fingered the square amulet hanging around his neck. Myldryd's half of the talisman lay buried in a grave far away. He whispered the words etched in delicate runes on its copper surface. "Think of me, I think of you. Love me, I love you."

This amulet did exist. Found in a Viking grave, it was one of the artifacts on display at the Royal British Columbia Museum in 2014.

VALKYRIES

The Valkyries chose half of the fallen warriors for the goddess Freyja. As well as the deity of love and fertility, she was also a battle goddess and chief of the Valkyries. She received the dead in her home, Fólkvangr, an Old Norse word which means *the Warrior Plain* or *the People's Field*.

In Old Norse literature little is said of Freyja's dwelling place and what awaited the dead warrior, although Fólkvangr has a beautiful hall called Sessrumne with many seats for fallen fighters.

Freyja is described as outspoken and, from a Christian point of view, immoral. Perhaps Christian chroniclers left out the stories of what happened in Fólkvangr and Sessrumne?

~courtesy of the Royal British Columbia Museum

ABOUT THE AUTHOR

Thank you for reading *The Rover Bold*. If you'd like to leave a review where you purchased the book, and/or on Goodreads, I would appreciate it.

I'd love you to visit my newly revamped website   at annamarkland.com and my Facebook page, Anna Markland Novels. Tweet me @annamarkland.

I was born and educated in England, but I've lived most of my life in Canada. I was an elementary school teacher for 25 years. It was a rewarding career, financially, spiritually and emotionally.

After that I worked with my husband in the management of his businesses. He's a born entrepreneur who likes to boast he's never had a job! (He's also of Norwegian ancestry and LOVES this story.)

My final "career" was as Director of Administration of a global disaster relief organization.

Not content to fade away into retirement gracefully, I embarked upon writing a romance, essentially for my own satisfaction. I chose the medieval period mainly because that genre of historical romance is one I enjoy reading.

I have a keen interest in genealogy. This hobby has had a tremendous influence on my stories. My medieval romances are about family honor, ancestry, and roots. As an amateur genealogist, I cherished a dream (as do many) of tracing my own English roots back to the Norman Conquest—an impossibility since I am not descended from nobility! So I made up a family and my stories follow its members through successive generations.

One of the things I enjoy most about writing historical romance is the in-depth research necessary to provide readers with an authentic medieval experience. I based the plot of my first novel, *Conquering Passion*, on an incident that actually happened to a Norman noblewoman.

I hope you come to know and love my cast of characters as much as I do.

I'd like to acknowledge the invaluable assistance of my critique partners in polishing this manuscript. Thank you Sylvie Grayson, Reggi Allder and Jacquie Biggar.

EXCERPT FROM THE ROVER DEFIANT

Rouen, Terra Normanorum, Francia, 912AD

Torstein's throat constricted as he stared at the squirming newborn in his arms.

"Don't be afraid," the babe's mother reassured him with a smile, "you won't drop your cousin."

Cousin!

Did he dare murmur the word? As a slave he'd never been acknowledged as a member of the Gardbruker family, though he was the child of one of their sons. But his mother had been a thrall.

His father, Gunnar, had been swept away in a storm tide the autumn before the Vikings left their Norwegian coastal village forever in search of a new life. His mother had been sold off with other slaves in the Danes' market at Ribe during the voyage from Møre to Francia. The chieftain had declared them dead weight.

"Don't worry," Cathryn said, still smiling, jolting him from his memories.

Torstein thought to tell his aunt-by-marriage that she looked serene, even after laboring for hours in the small chamber in the Archbishop of Rouen's house to bring forth her son. But he doubted his uncle would approve, despite his obvious euphoria at having sired a boy. It was evident he was uncomfortable with his nephew even holding the babe. Torstein was still amazed he'd been allowed into the chamber.

"He is beautiful," he ventured, inhaling the fresh scent of the new life he held. A lifetime of servile deference was difficult to forget, though his uncles had freed him months ago. It hadn't escaped his notice that many in the Viking community thought Bryk and Alfred had lost their wits when they'd granted him his freedom.

"Bah!" Bryk Kriger exclaimed impatiently, taking the squawking babe and holding him aloft. "Boys are not *beautiful*. They are handsome…sturdy…rugged."

Torstein felt the sudden absence of the child's warmth. The new babe threw his arms wide and wailed loudly, causing his father to laugh, but bringing a frown to his mother's brow.

If the boy grew to be like his father, he would indeed be big and strong, whereas Torstein had inherited his mother's frame and coloring. He was the only Gardbruker with dark hair and felt like a struggling sapling standing next to his uncles.

But a man didn't need muscles to be strong. Torstein might not be the celebrated warrior his uncle was, but he'd proven in the fight against the Frankish army he had as much Viking blood in his veins as any of them.

He'd led a revolt of slaves against their Frankish captors and helped his uncle rescue Cathryn from the enemy's clutches.

He wondered briefly if his dead father had felt the same pride and joy at his birth. But he knew the answer. Gunnar had barely acknowledged his existence. After the storm tide, his uncle Bryk had become his master.

Things might have gone on that way, but Odin had decreed otherwise. Though the battle against the Franks at Chartres had been lost, King Charles of Francia had conceded that the Vikings weren't going away and would continue to fight for land where they might settle. He'd granted their leader, Hrolf Ganger, control of a huge swath of the Seine valley, including the city of Rouen, in exchange for Hrolf's oath of fealty.

Hrolf in turn had given fertile land on the banks of the mighty river to Bryk and Alfred, and they had bestowed freedom on Torstein and recognized him as their nephew.

"What will you name him?" he rasped, suddenly uncomfortably aware of a jealous desire for a son of his own. As a thrall he'd sworn never to sire a child into slavery. But now—

Cathryn smiled again, her eyes full of love for her husband and the child he carried on his hip as if it were something he'd done all his life. Alfred had ten children, but this was Bryk's firstborn. Alfred's wife, Hannelore, had assisted Cathryn with the birth. "We decided on Bernhardt, after my father. Though I never knew him, I wish to honor his memory."

Torstein marveled that he often felt greater kinship with Cathryn, a Frank by birth, than with his own flesh and blood. But his aunt-by-marriage hadn't been raised a Viking and had made no secret of her abhorrence of the notion of slavery. Her generous heart had prompted the naming of her son after the father who'd drowned in the Seine before her birth. What would it be like to have such a woman look at him with adoration in her eyes?

Bryk's booming voice brought him back to the present. "But Magnus is the name he'll be known by. After my father."

My grandfather.

The realization jolted Torstein. He had only a vague memory of the giant warrior who'd somehow managed to go a-viking frequently and run a productive farm in Møre. He'd died in his sleep at a ripe old age. After his death Alfred and Gunnar had taken over the family farm and apple orchards.

Bryk had followed in his father's roving footsteps. But then he'd suddenly turned his back on murder and mayhem and joined his brothers. Most in Møre deemed him a coward for his actions. His first wife, Hrolf Ganger's sister, had died of shame. She'd taken their unborn child to the grave.

Torstein felt great joy for his uncle's newfound happiness. He'd at first agreed with the settlement's condemnation of Bryk Gardbruker. But he'd come to know his uncle as a man of great courage and strength, a hero deserving of the ballads the *skalds* sang of him around the campfires. He'd left Norway a *nithing*, but now Hrolf had recognized him as one of his most worthy and trusted lieutenants. Bryk Gardbruker had been renamed Bryk Kriger—the Farmer had become the Warrior.

Torstein's bravery at Chartres hadn't gone unnoticed by his fellow Vikings, but he could only hope one day to be as celebrated as his uncle. That might take a miracle.

The Frankish Christians often spoke in hushed tones of miracles wrought by the *Vite Krist*. Torstein had become an adherent of their faith, as had all the Vikings—the acceptance of the White Christ a condition imposed by King Charles the Senseless. But he had a feeling deep in his heart that entreaties to Freyja, goddess of fertility, might prove to be more productive if he embarked on a search for a wife.

His uncle handed a now screaming Magnus Bernhardt back to his mother. "He's hungry," he said in Norse, cocking his head towards Torstein. "Best you leave now."

A dangerous impulse to watch Cathryn suckle her child seized him. He thirsted for what Bryk had. He imagined his uncle's delight at watching his wife feed their son.

But Bryk would kill him if he even suspected Torstein harbored a notion to look upon Cathryn's breasts.

Not that he was interested in his aunt-by-marriage that way. As he'd grown to manhood in Norway, only one woman had caught his eye, and the interest of his *pikk*, but Sonja Karlsdatter was the daughter of a Viking nobleman from a neighboring settlement—she didn't know he existed.

OTHER BOOKS BY ANNA

Dear Reader,

If you'd like to know more about the descendants of The Rover Bold, here's a handy reference list.

Conquering Passion—Ram and Mabelle, Rhodri and Rhonwen
If Love Dares Enough—Hugh and Devona, Antoine and Sybilla
Defiant Passion-Rhodri and Rhonwen
A Man of Value—Caedmon and Agneta
Dark Irish Knight—Ronan and Rhoni
Haunted Knights—Adam and Rosamunda, Denis and Paulina
Passion in the Blood—Robert and Dorianne, Baudoin and Carys
Dark and Bright—Rhys and Annalise
The Winds of the Heavens—Rhun and Glain, Rhydderch and Isolda
Dance of Love—Izzy and Farah
Carried Away—Blythe and Dieter
Sweet Taste of Love—Aidan and Nolana
Wild Viking Princess—Ragna and Reider
Hearts and Crowns—Gallien and Peridotte
Fatal Truths—Alex and Elayne
Sinful Passions—Bronson and Grace, Rodrick and Swan

If you like stories with medieval breeds of dogs, you'll enjoy **If Love Dares Enough**, **Carried Away**, and **Wild Viking Princess**. If you have a soft spot for cats, read **Passion in the Blood** and **Haunted Knights**.

If you are looking for historical fiction set in a certain region:
English History—all books
Norman French History—all books
Crusades—A Man of Value
Welsh History—Conquering Passion, Defiant Passion, Dark and Bright, The Winds of the Heavens
Scottish History—Conquering Passion, A Man of Value, Sweet Taste of Love
European History (Holy Roman Empire)—Carried Away
Danish History—Wild Viking Princess
Spanish History—Dance of Love
Ireland—Dark Irish Knight

If you like to read about historical characters:
William the Conqueror—Conquering Passion, If Love Dares Enough, Defiant Passion
William Rufus—A Man of Value
Robert Curthose, Duke of Normandy—Passion in the Blood
Henry I of England—Passion in the Blood, Sweet Taste of Love, Haunted Knights, Hearts & Crowns
Heinrich V, Holy Roman Emperor—Carried Away
Vikings—Wild Viking Princess
Kings of Aragon (Spain)—Dance of Love
The Anarchy—Hearts and Crowns, Fatal Truths, Sinful Passions

Enjoy!

CPSIA information can be obtained
at www.ICGtesting.com
Printed in the USA
FSOW02n2358050715
8538FS